CW01081731

The Time Capture

Fiction by Annie Hoad

For 8-12 year olds

Tomb of the Crumbly Bones

Kali's First (Totally Magnificent) Chronicle

This daring, fun-filled adventure will make you gasp, giggle and hug your best friends tightly.

Reviews for Tomb of the Crumbly Bones on Amazon

"I read the book in less than a week because it was so exciting and I really wanted to know what happened next." *Caitlin - aged 8*

"Buy this book and enjoy being drawn into Kali's world!" *HS*

"This book is supposed to be for 8-12 years old I am way past that age but I couldn't put it down. It is easy light reading and thoroughly enjoyable. I have a lot of contact with kids this age and would recommend this book for them as well." *Rozchop*

The Time Capture

Annie Hoad

For Jude and Anne
And for all sisters
Everywhere

Text copyright © 2020 Annie Hoad
Cover art and illustrations copyright © 2020 Leo Martyn
All rights reserved.
ISBN-13: 9798654771629
All characters in this publication are fictitious and any resemblance to real
persons, living or dead is purely coincidental.

Table of Contents

1
The Welcome

In the winter months, Measles, my cat, likes to sleep on top of my head for warmth. I reach up sleepily and rub her velvet-soft ears then I check the clock beside my bed. 7.25 a.m.

Just ninety-five minutes until I start college and go through my first ever solo time capture. With no teachers to guide me, there's a real possibility that something unexpected or exciting might actually happen for the first time in my life. I've been waiting for this moment to arrive since I fell in love with captures, when I was six years old. But now that the big day is finally here, I'm suddenly not sure whether I've made the best decision of my life, or the worst. Based on the churned up sea-storm feeling in my stomach, my guts don't know the answer to that question either.

I push myself out of bed before first-day nerves can get an even tighter grip on me, and walk silently down the hall to the bathroom. Then I dress carefully, picking out clothes for comfort, a soft leaf-green jumper, my favourite jeans and pliable leather lace-up boots. No earrings or jewellery in case I get sent through a capture where speed and agility are required. Nothing can slow me down today.

Measles pads softly behind me as I grab my bag and creep down the hall again without waking my aunt, Yarena. I've lived with Yarena, my dad's sister, since my parents both died in a boating accident when I was two years old. Yarena has been my whole family for so long now that when I think of a mum, she's who I picture in a slightly fuzzy, out of focus kind of way. And we usually bump along together well enough. If she was awake right now she'd insist on making pancakes for breakfast, and there's no way I can get anything solid past the nervous constriction in my throat. She'd also send me straight back to my room to change into less battered boots, but these boots are trusted friends, solemates, so they're staying on my feet no matter what.

I open the front door, closing it gently behind me to avoid creaking hinges, and tread lightly down the corridor towards the stairs. It's much better this way, just me and my boots. I'll square things up with Yarena later, do the washing up, make her a cup of tea and tell her everything I want her to hear about college.

Yarena, Measles and me live on the fifth floor of the Cromwell Institute of Captured Time. Built a hundred and forty-one years ago in the centre of London, it's also the only home I've ever known. The vast Portland Stone building is intentionally grand and intimidating, so that no one can challenge the importance of Cassian Cromwell and his notion of captured time. But no one ever would. Time capture is so ingrained in the fabric of our world that it's as vital and unquestioned as sunshine.

Yarena has told me the story of Cassian Cromwell so many times over the years that it almost feels like part of our own history now. How the idea of time capture came to him in a fever-filled dream, when he was bedridden with such a severe case of the flu, that both Cassian and his doctors feared he might die. In his delirium, he was convinced he'd discovered how to capture any moment and hold onto it forever. So that every taste, smell, sight, sound, touch, thought and emotion, every ray of sunshine and drop of rain, atom for atom, molecule for molecule, could be caught and preserved so perfectly, that even the Gods themselves would be unable to tell the difference between a time capture, and the world it had been taken from. That's always been my favourite part of the whole story. Whenever I hear it, I like to imagine a Greek marble-statue of a God wandering through a field, trying to figure out from the sway of the grass and the flapping of bird wings whether he's inside a capture or not.

The vivid dream never left Cassian. And four decades after his brush with death, he finally created the world's first time capture. Taken on a peaceful stroll through the meadows behind his home, it meant that anyone could now meander through the same daisy-speckled field, that they could live through the exact moment when the capture was taken. To this day, it's still the most visited capture in history.

I've been through it three times already, twice with Yarena, once with my class at primary school when I was still a kid. I've also been to the Taj Mahal, the Great Pyramid of Giza and the Colosseum in Rome, as well as some of the early twenty-first century rocket launches at Cape Canaveral. But my favourite captures are the ones where people do crazy things, like taking a cold-sea swim on New Year's Day, in the Scottish town of Greenock, where your skin turns so icy it literally feels like it's burning. I also love some of the old captures taken at random places and times around the globe, capturing a snapshot of everyday life from long ago, from inside people's homes, schools, work places, chess clubs, theatres and supermarkets, where you could buy something called *Farm Fresh Cowsticks* that were made from reconstituted meat slurry. I still can't figure out if that's a joke, or if people actually ate them for real. One day, I'll pluck up enough courage to take a bite and see for myself — maybe.

Captures can be bizarre, beautiful, awe-inspiring and life-changing, and I've loved them with the deepest parts of my soul since I was six years old. But they can also be deadly.

Want to know what it feels like to set foot on Mars? Go ahead, explore the red planet, see the genuine dust on your shoes and marvel at the sight of the sun, seen from an entirely different point in the solar system. But make sure you wear a proper survival suit with an adequate supply of oxygen, or you will suffocate, or freeze to death, in exactly the same time it would take to do so on the surface of the actual planet.

According to official statistics, the number of people who have lost their lives inside captures over the last century alone is ninety-one.

My sister, Millie Hummingtree, was one of them.

Sent to explore a remote mountain region in South America, she was struck by a sudden rockslide and killed along with several other capture volunteers. I was only nine years old at the time. My memories of her are confused, patchy and fleeting, but they're also intense. I can remember the wet October day when we built a tent in my room, using the sheets and blankets from my bed, glow-in-the-dark stars stuck to the peaked ceiling with flour paste. I also remember the time we baked a cake for Yarena's birthday, and somehow managed to cover the entire kitchen floor in cocoa powder, which turned into a muddy lake the instant we tried to mop it up. This I remember clearly, along with the fact that Millie then laid on the floor scooping out big, glorious mud angels, her arms and legs sweeping through the mess we'd made. But no matter how hard I try, I cannot recall the day my sister died.

Sometimes, I like to imagine Millie's still here with me, in this world, playing an endless game of hide-and-seek that I can never win, like she's still alive in the shadows. Or that she's sitting on the end of my bed when I wake in the night, and I swear I can practically feel the comforting lean of her warm body tucked in against mine. On days like today, I can easily conjure up a glimpse of her walking beside me, teasing me about the love I have for my boots, throwing a big-sister arm around my shoulders to stop me from trembling with nerves. I'm grateful for the illusion, because between Millie's shadow and my boots, I'm never entirely alone, and I need them both badly today.

I hurry down four flights of stairs, feeling sicker with every step. I swipe through the door at the bottom with my resident's pass, and enter the Long Walk, a white-walled thoroughfare that spans the full width of the building. It's already filling up with administrators who deal with the day-to-day running of the Institute, en route to their offices on the second and third floors. I push my way through the human bottleneck that has gathered outside a bank of mirrored lifts, and head for the far end where an internal entrance to the adjoining building, the Cromwell College of Captology, awaits. I cross the threshold with a slight tug of hesitation, almost expecting something inside me to flip and change, because this is where the rest of my life begins. I'm not certain if I'm ready for that life yet, but it's too late to drop out of the course now, even though I've considered doing just that about a million times in the last week alone.

I head straight up the stairs to the cafeteria on the fifth floor. This part of the college is filled with light and air. Huge, sloping, floor-to-ceiling windows reveal glimpses of the city all the way down to the river, the muddy colour of which reminds me of the cocoa incident again, and I allow myself one small smile. The Capital Building rises through a thin layer of morning mist, it sits next to the ancient Tower of London which somehow holds its own beside the brash, bullying structures trying to crowd it out. On the far wall of the cafeteria, a large screen shows the latest scandals caught on capture; the son of a billionaire and his jewel-thieving compulsion, the movie star and his latest affair, the female politician blowing millions of pounds of public money on luxury yachts and fake tans, with added gold-leaf sparkle.

I scan the tables and the long line already forming at the food counter searching for Hekla. She's sitting by a window, arms folded, eyes closed, feet resting on the seat opposite with her usual air of ownership.

"It's about time," she says as I approach, her eyes still shut. "I've been waiting for ages, what took you so long?"

Hekla McKellor has been my best friend since our first year at primary school. Her long straight blond hair comes from her Icelandic mother, her slight frame and inquisitive eyes from her Scottish-Indian father. Even in a city as diverse as London, Hekla stands out, but that could also have something to do with the silver skull rings she wears through her ears, and on every one of her fingers. And the bright red patent-leather ankle boots that she never takes off. Her taste in clashing colours could teach circus clowns something about getting noticed.

"I had to scare off some pimply-faced geek and his friends to get this table," Hekla says, finally opening her eyes. She swings her legs to one side so I can sit down next to the window.

"When did you really get here?" I ask, helping myself to one of four iced pastries heaped onto a plate in front of her.

Hekla shrugs. "Ten minutes ago, didn't want to be late on our first day."

I grip the inside of my boots with my toes and place the pastry back on the pile, wondering how I could have considered eating it.

It's traditional for every new student at the Cromwell College to start their course by going through a pure moment of captured time. It could be anything, a breezy day at the beach, the departure lounge at a busy airport, a noisy market in Marrakesh or a ride on an ancient steam train. Each student goes through a completely different capture, chosen from an archive of millions. None will be rated above U for Universal, which means nothing dangerous, sinister, creepy, disturbing or potentially life-threatening. But I can't help feeling anxious at the thought of what my capture will be. I've been through many before, everyone has. All school children in the capital come to the Institute at least once a year, for guided walks through ancient Roman ruins, or bat-filled caves, or scorching deserts, everything safe, controlled and danger free. But nothing will compare with this moment, when I walk alone for the first time, finally considered old enough to deal with whatever I might find.

"I hope I get to feed the tigers at one of those safari parks," Hekla says, almost reading my thoughts.

"You hate animals," I say, picking at a pastry, hoping the sweet sticky glaze might help take the edge off my nerves. "You almost had a panic attack when we went to feed the pigs at that city farm back in year six."

"Yeah, but I'd rather get pigs than some dog-grooming salon."

I can't help grinning.

"Imagine coming out of your first capture and having to tell everyone you've been watching some Cockapoo getting its toenails clipped."

Hekla in a dog-grooming salon? The image makes me smile until my face aches. The two things she hates most in the world are being outdoors and any animal over the size of a hamster. She prefers the predictable behaviours of computers and electronic gadgets to almost anything else, and she begins her own course today as a capture technician. Technicians are responsible for designing the highly sophisticated and top-secret technology that enables us to capture time, and for pushing that technology in new and exciting directions. They're always entry-level genius and generally consider themselves to be a much higher level of human being than any mere captologist. But captologists do all the real work, searching for the magical and unexpected, trekking to the wild places of the world where shooting stars still race each other across dark skies, where doomsday storms skim the horizon, blotting out the sun, witnessed only by ancient trees and the beetles that burrow beneath their roots. That's what I hope to capture one day, if I'm ever good enough. I finally stop grinning, feeling sick again.

For the first time in ten years, me and Hekla will be separated by the different choices we've made. The thought adds yet another twist to the knots in my stomach. I don't make friends easily. It took two solid months of sitting next to Hekla at school before I plucked up enough courage to talk to her. Another three before we could truly be classed as friends. And that was only because Hekla had already made up her mind about me, and refused to let me shy away from her whispered comments and jokes. Being fifteen has not made the process any easier for me. I already know I won't speak to anyone today unless I'm forced into it.

"I still think you're certifiably crazy for wanting to be a captologist," Hekla says, rubbing a speck of dirt off her precious boots with her sleeve. "Everyone's going to compare you to your sister."

"Everyone already does," I point out truthfully.

It doesn't help that I'm a carbon copy of Millie. I have the same tall, slightly willowy build, bordering on the gangly, the same green eyes, the same silvery hair, a genetic mutation from our dad's side of the family that makes me stand out even more easily. I'm like a walking moonbeam. So I guess the comparisons are inevitable and I've heard them all before.

"You look so much like your sister...sound so much like your sister...remind me so much of your sister...should be so proud of your sister..."

I don't blame Millie; it's not her fault that she was born first. But she left behind such a swamp of comparison for me to wade through, that sometimes, I can't help wishing I'd been born with crow-black hair, or blue eyes, or a face full of freckles, anything to mark me out as different, to make people see that we are not the same. Especially now, when I'm about to blur the lines even further, to train as a captologist when Millie has already gone before me, a capture volunteer, exploring the dangerous and unusual, until it killed her.

I sigh heavily, wondering for the thousandth time if I should have stayed at school for another few years, and then gone to university to study conservation or geography or plumbing instead. But that would have forced me to bury my own dreams and ambitions. At least *I'm almost sure* they're my ambitions. Sometimes, even I have trouble figuring out where Millie ends and I begin. Does my desire to work with captured time stem from a shared gene pool with my sister, or from a totally unique place inside me? That's what I'm hoping to find out, to resolve the never-ending internal argument before it drives me totally insane. How could I have reached the age of fifteen without knowing the answer to this question? If the answer already exists inside me, it's camouflaging itself with the skill of a cuttle fish in a seaweed patch.

Hekla bolts down two pastries and a mug of cold tea before we finally leave the cafeteria. The college stairwells and corridors are now clogged with older students, all setting out their claims for the best lockers and places to meet, the noise levels swelling as they greet old friends. It takes us ten minutes to weave our way through the different groups and reach the third floor, which is filled with banks of capture booths, and a massive repository for training captures. We join the back of a long queue that stretches the full length of a featureless corridor and wait.

I only recognise a few faces from our old school in the city. All other students have come from different parts of the country. Places on the capture courses are highly sort after and are only awarded to those who managed to score ninety percent, or above, in a series of entrance exams and interviews that were so gruelling, they left me with an ugly hyperventilation problem. Hekla sailed through every test coming out in the top percentile of the whole intake. I am sitting somewhere in the middle, not good enough to be noticed by anyone yet, other than for the obvious reasons.

Hekla jokes around as we inch forward, easy in her own skin, enviably sure of her own talents, even if they do place her dangerously close to the geek faction that she loves to mock and tease. By the time we reach the front of the queue, my hands are so clammy I have to wipe them the full length of my jeans to remove the slick of sweat. When we approach a counter, a bored-looking woman with salt-and-pepper hair and glasses checks our names against a list on her computer screen.

"Hekla McKellor, booth number twelve," she says, pointing down a corridor to the left, without looking up. "Kaida Hummingtree." This time she pauses and glances in my direction, recognising the surname, instantly spotting the resemblance between me and my sister. She nods as if acknowledging who I am. "Hummingtree, you're in twenty-seven. Emergency door release buttons are on the inside wall marked For Emergency Use Only, if you are injured and need assistance, wait for someone to come to you. In the event of a panic attack, sit on the floor of your booth, breathe deeply and picture a happy place," she says severely, looking like she's never pictured a happy place in her life. She also rattles off an endless list of warnings and instructions. Hekla pulls a face at the mention of procedures for mopping up our own vomit. "When your capture has finished, exit the booth *immediately* so that other students may use it. *Do not* make me come in there and drag you out because you're having such a marvellous time, you've decided to go through the capture again."

"Scary!" Hekla mouths as she peels off to the left with a carefree wave. "Meet you in the cafeteria for lunch?"

I swallow with difficulty. "Can you please stop talking about food?"

Hekla smiles and blows me a long string of big showy kisses, like she always does when she knows I'm struggling with nerves. "Have a good capture. Try not to pee your pants!"

I'm not making any promises I can't keep. I head down my own corridor with a lot less confidence and swagger, hoping my boots will keep me moving in the right direction if my courage fails.

Dimmed floor lights guide me past a row of tall, opaque, glass-fronted booths, all occupied, all illuminated from within by the captures being played out inside them. Number twenty-seven is dark but I know how this

8

works. I try to ignore what now feels like a fish flapping around inside my stomach, grab the handle and open the door. It leads straight into a cramped changing room with a bench for putting on boots, skis, or flippers as needed, and a row of pegs for clothes. Beside an inner glass door is a screen where the contents of the capture are usually displayed, date, time, location, temperature, special conditions. But this screen is blank. A green light flashes on above the door, a sign that it's now safe to enter. I hesitate, wondering if I should report the faulty screen to the woman at the desk, then I decide to see for myself first.

As I pull the inner door open and step inside, my heart rate triples. It takes several seconds for my eyes to adjust to the low light levels, but I can see the booth is about the size of one of the classrooms at my last school, with a high ceiling and slightly greasy-looking walls. Things have been ground up, smashed to pieces and driven to extinction over and over inside this booth. There's also a faint, lingering aroma of wood smoke, a remnant from the last capture, which makes me think of bonfires.

When I suddenly see Cassian Cromwell walking towards me moments later, I have to batten down an impulse to hide, knowing that the scary desk woman could be watching me on a monitor, knowing that I am likely to be under more scrutiny than any other student starting here today. I'm the sister of Millie Hummingtree, star volunteer and darling of the Institute, every teacher, student and scary desk woman in the entire college will be wondering if I have even a tenth of her natural talent. I'm more anxious than anyone to find the answer to that question.

The Cassian Cromwell in my capture is a direct descendant of the great man who first discovered how to capture time; he's the current custodian of the Institutes in London, New York, Wellington, Delhi, Cape Town, Moscow and Beijing. He's also one of the most powerful men in the world and although I live in his Institute, I've never met him before.

I automatically run a hand over my hair, smoothing the seams straight on my jumper. I know this is just a standard welcome capture, probably taken weeks, or maybe even months ago, but at this moment, I'm still standing in the presence of the real Cassian Cromwell.

Every thought in his head, every red blood cell racing around his body, has been preserved exactly as it was at this point in time. If he'd eaten a ripe peach just before this capture was taken, and I shook his hand right now, I'd feel the sweet stickiness of the fruit transfer from his skin to mine.

"Welcome to the Cromwell College of Captology," Cassian says in the easy, melodic voice I've heard so many times before on news clips. He's dressed in a smart grey tweed suit, his olive-toned skin has a healthy glow as if he's just come back from a holiday at his Italian villa. Every facet of his life has been picked over by the media since the day he was born, down to the name of his tailor and the shoe size of his daughter, Olivia. But the one thing I knew nothing about until this moment was his natural charm and charisma; it feels like he could move any mountain, stop any clock from ticking with an easy lift of his smile. He stands several feet away from me but I can still see the amber flecks in his eyes.

"The fact that you are standing before me now means you've earned your place in our history, and a place on one of our prestigious courses. You are about to join a very large but close-knit family of captologists, so crucial to the running of this Institute."

That's one of the things I love most about this place, it's still run like a family business. When Cassian first established the Institute, he made it clear that no capture would ever be taken for profit. No government, bank, pharmaceutical company or global corporation could ever pay for the privilege. All captologists remain in the employment of the Cromwell Institute, and the Cromwells decide where each capture should be taken, and for what purpose. The Cromwells have still amassed an obscene fortune by selling broadcasting rights for the most important, historic or gossip-worthy captures. But nobody tells the Cromwells what to do.

"On behalf of the entire Cromwell family, past, present and future," Cassian continues, "may I wish you good luck in your endeavours, and I hope you will find your time with us challenging and rewarding."

With one final smile, he turns and retreats into the distance leaving nothing behind but the exquisite scent of warm citrus. The air inside the booth now feels charged and full of potential, and I know that my own personal capture is about to begin. This is the moment I've been dreaming about since I was six years old. I drag several long gulps of air down to the bottom of my lungs, trying to stay grounded in my boots, dry in my pants. The change happens slowly, light levels lifting around me to reveal a different floor, walls and ceiling. It takes me less than six seconds to realise where I'm standing, and it's literally the last place on this, or any other planet, that I expected to find myself at this moment.

2
LoveNature
Eternal

I reach out and brush familiar wood-panelled walls, smooth and warm feeling beneath my fingertips. There's a comforting smell of burnt toast in the air and a faded green rug beneath my feet, the same rug I crept across less than two hours ago, trying not to wake Yarena. For my first ever solo time capture, I've been sent to the one place I know better than any other. I'm standing in my own hallway at home.

I hesitate, flustered with indecision, wondering if the capture booth is faulty after all. Or maybe this is how the college tutors inform middling students, like me, that they've decided to give your place on the course to someone with more talent, that you're fit for nothing more challenging than a visit to your own home. I walk slowly down the hall trying not to let my confusion and disappointment show, past the open bathroom door, past Millie's old room which still smells of the fruity lip balm that she loved so much.

Pale winter sunlight hits me as soon as I enter the living space. Like all flats on this floor of the Institute, the kitchen, dining area and sitting room are contained within one large open-plan space. Tall floor-to-ceiling windows look out to the horizon, framing a living London mural of high-rise office blocks and low-rise historical landmarks that I love to pick out, like characters from a favourite book. In the room itself, everything is exactly as it should be, the worn brown sofa with its sagging, bottom-shaped indentations, Yarena's collection of stout blue ceramic vases and the living tree in the far corner, decorated with crystal teardrops that spin lazily, sending sun-flickers around the room. Everything is familiar and comforting, home. So why am I here?

I glance at the small red calendar clock on the wall. It tells me that this capture was taken at 8.15 a.m. exactly two days ago. Captures are usually only taken inside private dwellings for the social archives, to show how we live, what clothes we wear, what food we eat, how we speak to each other in the language and attitudes of the era. But they are only ever taken with the homeowner's permission. Yarena is a quiet, private person, she would never agree to such an intrusion, even for the archives. The only other reason a capture is ever taken inside someone's home, is when the police suspect that a crime is about to be committed.

Measles suddenly rushes past my legs making me flinch. I reach out to stroke her soft fur, dotted with the black measles she was named after, but I can tell she doesn't feel the pressure of my hand. This capture has been set in observation mode, which means I can't interact with any living creatures I encounter, human or feline, my presence cannot be felt.

I follow Measles further into the living space looking for any clues as to why a capture might have been taken here, just two days ago. It was a Saturday. I think hard trying to remember exactly what happened at 8.15 a.m. Yarena went out early to meet some friends for breakfast and then shopping. I spent the morning on my own in the flat, reading, daydreaming about my first day at college, hunting through a pile of discarded clothes in my room for my favourite pink socks. No crimes were committed. No one came to the door or sent any messages via LondonCall.

I turn slowly, feeling mystified, staring at each section of the room for anything out of place or unusual. Nothing. But I hear a faint noise coming from the kitchen. It sounds like a chair being scraped across the floor. I freeze, instinctively worried about what I might find if I go and investigate, even though I know all of this is history, and reason tells me I won't find anything. Nothing happened at this moment on Saturday morning. I should know; I've already lived through it once.

I walk slowly past the tall wooden cupboards that separate the kitchen from the living area, instantly finding the source of the noise.

It's me. Kaida Hummingtree.

I take a hasty step backwards, a hand covering my mouth. The sight of myself is somehow more shocking than discovering a monkey rifling through the fridge for bananas. I stand and gaze, caught somewhere between fascination and squirming. This is the same body I exist in everyday, down to the single freckle on my nose, and the faint scar on the back of my hand, where I once got tangled up in a barbed wire fence. If I looked through the pockets in my jeans, the ones that the other me is wearing, I know I'd find a heart-shaped key ring and a stub of pencil, pale blue. My eyes look overly bright, my expression determined and serious. It's clear that green is a colour I should only wear on the lower half of my body, as next to the skin on my face and neck, it casts an unflattering hue of dead vegetation that nobody has ever bothered telling me about. I look shorter; my body even more awkward than it appears to me in every mirror.

I watch myself as I tie my hair off my face, securing it with two pins, and pull a coat on over one of my favourite sweatshirts. Then I take a step closer, frowning. I haven't worn that particular sweatshirt in weeks, after I accidentally splattered the sleeve with hot chilli sauce. The stain stubbornly refused to come out, no matter how many times I washed it, and I eventually abandoned the sweatshirt to the dark recesses of my wardrobe. I also know for a fact that on Saturday morning, just two days ago, I spent practically the whole day in my favourite octopus-patterned pyjamas. It was bitterly cold outside, cold enough for the river Thames to freeze over, for the Westminster Ice Gardens to open their gates for the first time all winter. It was also too cold in our ancient bathroom to take a shower or wash my hair, so I didn't even bother getting dressed until Yarena came home in the middle of the afternoon. But there's no time to question these strange inconsistencies now, because this girl is suddenly picking up an old rucksack and heading for the door.

Without hesitation I follow. For a fleeting moment it crosses my mind that this might be some kind of practical joke, a student prank meant to fool and embarrass me on my first day of college. But even that's impossible.

Captures cannot be fabricated. You can't sit in your bedroom at home and simply conjure one up on your computer. Nor can they be altered. Everything is as set in stone as a fossilised fish in an ancient riverbed. It's not possible to make them show anything other than what they captured at the time. It's one of the main reasons why they're so valued, so important to our society.

Want to know what it really felt like to take part in the historic anti-tree-felling protests, in the early part of the century? Just immerse yourself in one of the captures taken at the time, with the absolute certainty that every detail is one hundred percent authentic and real, down to the composition of the pollen that drifts through the air, and the grime underneath the fingernails of the protestors.

Never seen a real criminal trial before? Come to the Cromwell Institute of Captured Time and sit among the jury as they decide the fate of the accused, or feel the tension, raw and emotional, from the public gallery as the verdict is announced. Captures are used to convict the guilty and free the innocent because they show the absolute, unalterable truth in any situation.

Except for now, I realise.

Because I am watching this person, who is clearly supposed to be me down to the blood and bones, do things I never did. I never left the flat on Saturday and yet this girl, this imposter, evil-twin me, is closing the front door and hurrying down the stairs towards the Long Walk. How can any of this be happening?

I keep my distance, worried that my presence will somehow be felt, but nothing I do can alter this capture. It's already in the past, an assumed fact. The girl heads down the empty Long Walk and then veers off suddenly into the main concourse of the Institute, using my resident's pass to swipe in through an internal door. It's still too early for this section of the Institute to be open to the public, if there are any cleaners or maintenance staff around I don't see them as I trail behind the girl. For a moment, we both stop and stare at the magnificent space. The whole place has an opulent feel, an old-world glamour with its cut-glass chandeliers, cool marble floors and towering columns. Indoor trees create shade on hot summer days, and living sculptures in the long winter months.

Most people come to the Institute to visit one of the four vast capture booths in this part of the building, that are open to anyone for the price of a ticket. Yarena has taken me to all the momentous events held here since I was little, including dog sledding through snowbound woods in Lapland, and a zip wire ride over the lush, dense treetops in the New Zealand bush. Once, we even took a midnight candlelit tour of the great palace at Versailles, and I still remember the strong smell of faded, decadent history that seemed to seep into my clothes and linger there for days afterwards. Some of the happiest moments of my life so far have been spent in this part of the Institute. But this definitely isn't one of them.

The girl turns towards the nearest capture booth, which is currently offering a two hour camel trek across the deserts of the Sahara — feel the

14

warm wind as it caresses your cheek, smell the filthy stench of camel hair as it sticks unpleasantly to your skin. Then she moves onto a collection of smaller booths, where visitors can experience the captures they've requested from the archives for history projects, or for family reunions with great-great-Grandpa and Grandma, or for thrill seeking escapades over white-water rapids, if they're old enough to request them.

The girl hovers nervously for a minute before a glass case with a display of historic capture machines, the first ever created, their simple box-like structure concealing the miracles of particle physics and advanced technology that allow time to be captured. Only a handful of people have ever seen what's inside one of those hallowed boxes. Although plenty have tried to steal their secrets in the past, including the thief who took a capture machine from this very display, over six years ago now. The girl lingers by the display as if trying to decide something, and then she turns quickly and enters the Long Walk, forcing me to follow once again. At this time on a Saturday morning it's completely deserted, but she pauses guiltily, checking over her shoulder before taking another pass from her coat pocket. I'm close enough to read the name on the front. *Yarena Hummingtree.* I swallow hard. Passes stay with you for a lifetime; they're as personal as a diary or the family contacts on your phone. Stealing someone else's pass is worse than using their toothbrush or wearing their favourite socks without permission; it's a complete violation, crossing a line that most people would never dream of crossing. Whoever this girl is, we do not share the same DNA.

The girl swipes through a door marked *Archives, Research, Tech Labs and Subterranean Booths* and disappears inside. I run, slipping through the door before it closes, locking me out of whatever happens next. But I'm tempted to find the emergency stop button on the wall of the capture booth that I'm still in, because I'm not sure I want to go any further. Access to this part of the Institute is restricted and off-limits to everyone except the people who work down in the subterranean levels. I'm not supposed to be here. But Yarena has been an archivist at the Institute for almost twenty years, a senior archivist for the last ten. This is the route she takes to work every day, through the security door and down a narrow corridor lit by fluted wall lights. I've only been down this corridor twice before. Once on a school trip when I was ten, to see where all the captures are stored, and once only eight months ago on a *Take Your Grumpy Teenager*

To Work Day. On that occasion, I complained loudly about having to spend seven hours down in the sublevels, no sunlight, no fresh air. I sat in Yarena's cramped office as she catalogued a pile of captures, which I found almost as thrilling as watching dust settle on the carpet. But I now wish I'd paid more attention because I might have some idea about what all of this is leading to, which part of the sublevels this girl is apparently so determined to reach.

I follow her down five flights of stairs and squeeze through another security door at the bottom before it snaps shut. Both me and the girl are now standing in the vast confusing labyrinth of the archives. Tunnelled deep beneath the Institute, it's like entering a grey underground city with bare bedrock walls, where the last one hundred and sixty years of human history have been neatly labelled and tidied away. It's stuffy in this part of the building; the air smells like it's already passed through the disease-riddled lungs of someone with consumption. I hate the staleness, and the fact that this girl is forcing me to breathe it in.

I follow her as she heads past dark archive rooms on the left and right, so clearly this isn't a random search; she's here for something specific. She ducks into a small nook suddenly and I recognise it from my day here with Yarena, it holds nothing but a chair and a desk, on top of which sits a powerful computer with a large screen. The computer stores the Infinite Catalogue, which is a record of every capture ever taken, anywhere in this world and beyond. The capture that I'm currently playing a starring role in will already be part of the catalogue. I wonder for a moment what headings it has been indexed under, security risk, law breaker, troublemaker, because breaking into the archives is definitely against the law, and one of the stupidest things anyone could ever do. The real me would never consider doing anything so completely guaranteed to generate a criminal record.

The girl checks over her shoulder, determination written all over her painfully familiar face. She sits at the desk and taps two words into the keyboard that leave me feeling even more troubled and confused. *LoveNature Eternal*. It's the name of a not-for-profit organisation which helps preserve important landscapes and ecosystems around the world. LoveNature Eternal is also the very organisation I hope the Cromwell Institute will allow me to take captures for, one day, when I'm fully qualified.

The imposter girl prints off three reference numbers and I recognise every one, I know them so well in fact, I could pick them out of a thousand almost identical capture numbers in any police line-up.

LNE-C897-2167
LNE-C960-2140
LNE-C345-2069

Each one refers to a famous LoveNature Eternal capture showing some of the most extraordinary natural phenomena ever seen; a total solar eclipse, an impressive display of aurora borealis over the pitted landscape of Iceland and a giant permafrost explosion. For years now, I've been desperate to experience these very wonders for myself, which is why I have a matching list of numbers, large and bold, pinned to my bedroom wall like an admission of guilt. Bile rises up into my throat but I'm forced to swallow the bitterness down, because this ordeal isn't over yet.

The girl grabs the sheet of paper and doubles back into the labyrinth again. She enters archive number sixteen, it's huge, easily the size of an old factory, and kept at a very chilly five degrees Celsius to help preserve the captures. It's also dimly lit for the same reason, but the girl has a torch and a visitor's map — two more admissions of guilt. The shelves are arranged in military-like rows reaching all the way up to the high ceiling, holding nothing but the sleek black carbon-fibre canisters that all captures are contained within. It looks like a warehouse for giant beetles. Luminous reference numbers on the end of each shelf stack are the only way to navigate this maze. The girl hurries down the left-hand side of the room and stops about halfway down. By the time I've caught up with her, she's already grabbed one canister from the smooth cradle that it sits in, and slipped it into her bag.

This whole thing has now got way out of control. I wish I could warn the girl, tell her to use the abnormally large amounts of common sense that I know she's got, turn back, leave the captures, go home and lock the door. But this has already happened, there's nothing I can do to stop the consequences that will surely follow. It's precisely the reason why this particular capture was selected for me, I realise, feeling bile rise up into my throat again. Capture theft is a major crime. And this is my trial. No judge or jury are ever needed when a crime has been caught entirely on capture. As far as the world is concerned, I am already guilty. The whole thing looks so well thought out and deliberate, as if the girl, me, has been planning this theft for some time. All that's missing is a signed confession sitting neatly on my bed.

The girl takes two more canisters and then retraces her steps through the archives, using the stolen ID to zip through both security doors until she reaches the Long Walk again. She continues up to the fifth floor of the Institute and enters through the front door of the flat, without a backward glance or any signs of regret. I drag my feet, following at a greater distance, trying to delay the inevitable now that this fantasy is clearly coming to an end. I'm certain there'll be nothing else to see. I stand for a moment trying not to blame my boots for failing to keep me safe in my first solo capture, trying not to be sick outside my own front door, then I follow the girl into the flat, ending up exactly where I began less than an hour ago.

I fumble along the wall until I find the handle to the capture booth, and let myself back into the small room outside, which is no longer empty. A sallow-faced man is waiting for me. Dressed in an ill-fitting suit that smells of stale cooking fat, he seems to fill the entire space like an odour.

"Kaida Hummingtree?" he asks, with a disapproving twitch underneath his left eye. "Come with me, please."

"Where are we going?" I ask, hearing how frail and guilty my voice sounds.

"Someone wants to speak to you about the capture you've just experienced."

And I know it. My life is over. I've defiled the name of Hummingtree, the memory of my dead sister now forever stained by my supposed actions.

I follow the man out of the room and dig my nails into my clenched palms, trying to halt the fear and panic that are rising up inside me.

3
Promise

I keep my head down, eyes fixed on the floor, as I follow Cooking Fat past the queue of students still waiting for their turn in the booths. My skin burns with shame at the thought of how many of them might recognise my silvery hair, and I deliberately avoid looking at the scary desk woman. I don't want to see any disappointment on her face or accusation in her eyes. The man heads back up the stairs to the fourth floor of the college where most of the staff offices are situated. Open doors reveal cluttered, poky rooms, half submerged under piles of books and student papers, like freshly exposed layers of soil at an archaeological dig. As we reach the far end, the decor changes, wooden boards give way to thick tufted carpets, potted plants and bevel-edged picture frames. I swallow down hard. This walk only has one end. We're heading straight for the office of Aldora Scrim, college principal and master of my immediate fate. I glance down at my battered boots, wishing I'd chosen a newer pair after all, as if the boots are somehow a reflection of my tainted soul.

"Find a chair and wait here until you're called," the man says, as we reach a small seating area, beyond which there's only one door.

I sit heavily in a hard chair and try to assess the reality of my situation. Scrim does not waste her time dealing with petty student misdemeanours or disputes. She is my firing squad, my one-way ticket to the oblivion of the guilty. This is as far as my career as a captologist might ever go. But there is also one small flicker of hope at the end of this dismal tunnel. Aldora Scrim knew my mum and dad, who both worked at the Institute; I suppose it's kind of a family tradition. Mum was one of the guides who took people through the big public capture booths downstairs. Dad worked in the sublevel tech labs doing something complicated with atoms and molecules, although I've never found out what. Aldora Scrim has remained a close family friend in all the years since they died. I've seen her in the flat many times, with her shoes kicked off, a glass of wine in hand, trading gossip with Yarena about the people they both work with. She came to Millie's sixteenth birthday party with an extravagant, three-tiered chocolate cake. If she has any real loyalty to my family, then maybe she can pull some strings. Maybe there's some way I can convince her that I am the victim of a crime, and not the perpetrator. It's the only way I might end this day with my life still intact.

It takes me a moment to realise that I'm not the only person waiting outside her office. Half a dozen of the seats are already occupied, but no one attempts to catch my eye, or offer a smile or a word of encouragement. Everyone has the same solemn expression, I notice, doing a quick inventory of my fellow detainees. There's a girl, seventeen maybe, with faded pink hair. Draped across her chair with her long legs stretching out, she's invading the personal space of the boy sitting in front of her. Another boy with a heavy frown and even heavier eyebrows that meet in the middle sits forward, clenching and unclenching his fists, with obvious anger. Several of the detainees look petrified; one has tears rolling down his face, mingling with a string of slippery snot that flows freely from his nose. I wonder if they're all here for the same reason as me.

The door to Scrim's office opens and the sniveller is summoned inside. The pink-haired girl and the boy with the mono-brow are called in quick succession after that. Nobody comes back out again; nobody else arrives at the seats. I play with the idea of making a run for it, what if I just stood up and walked away? There's no sign of Cooking Fat, nothing to stop me from leaving the building. I could hide in one of the seedier parts of the city, down by the docks or the place where the old train lines converge and wild plants have reclaimed the tracks, turning it into an inner-city jungle. I could even get a message to Hekla, but then what? I have no money, nowhere to stay, no way of clearing my name. The only hunting for food I've ever done is through the sugar-coated aisles of my favourite bakery, but I can't exactly live off muffins. Well, not for long anyway.

"Kaida?" A short woman with a clipboard is standing at the open door beckoning me towards her, shattering my imaginary escape plans. It's time to plead my innocence. The only proof I have is a sauce-stained sweatshirt sitting in my wardrobe, but will it be enough to convince anyone, even an old family friend, that the impossible has just happened? I get to my feet shakily and follow the clipboard woman inside, wondering if I'm suffering from some rare and strange reaction to my first solo time capture, a reaction that causes vivid hallucinations. Maybe someone will escort me to a hospital ward where they can fix everything with a therapy session and a warm blanket.

Scrim's office is generous and richly furnished, with a heavy desk sitting in front of a tall half-moon window. I notice a glass decanter filled with amber liquid, a shoal of silver pens glimmering under the light of a soft lamp, the smell of polish. There are no therapists waiting with blankets. Four people sit behind the desk but my eyes hone in on Aldora Scrim, easily recognisable with her sapphire-blue eyes and thick white hair, cut short over her ears. College principal for the last fifteen years, she has been popular and efficient, an essential cog in the giant wheel that makes the whole Institute run seamlessly.

"Case number C27N90," the clipboard woman says clearly, as we stop in front of the firing squad. A hush falls and now everyone is watching me with curiosity. I was right about being under scrutiny, but this is not what I'd imagined.

It takes Aldora Scrim seven seconds to register my unexpected presence and then she's on her feet, leaning towards me, knuckles pressed hard into the desk. "Kaida?" She squeezes hurriedly past the others and takes me by the arm, leading me over to the far side of the room for privacy. She's dressed in a well-cut suit that shows she has kept herself in good shape. Her blood-red nail polish compliments the blue of her eyes, which are now searching my face for answers. "Kaida, what on earth are you doing here?"

I suddenly have no idea how to explain the bizarre events which have led to this meeting. "I've just been through my first solo capture," I say with some difficulty, as my brain has also decided this is the perfect moment to have a breakdown, and I'm now struggling to hold back a tsunami of anxiety and tears. "It showed me going down to the archives, but it was a fake."

Aldora Scrim frowns. "I don't understand; who brought you here?"

"The capture showed me stealing from the archives," I say, ignoring her question, determined to get my side of the story across before anyone else can intervene. "But I didn't, I swear I haven't taken anything!"

Scrim finally seems to understand that something is seriously wrong and she turns away from me, considering. "Gentlemen," she addresses the three men sitting behind her desk with a tone of absolute authority. "If you could leave us for a moment, please? This is a delicate matter, and I require some time alone with the accused."

The word shoots through me like I've just been plugged into the college mains, but that's exactly what I am now, guilty until proven innocent. I hang my head, like I've already been convicted, as the men shuffle out of their seats and leave the office, talking in low voices. But the stern clipboard woman remains. Scrim turns to her with a curt nod as soon as we have the room to ourselves. "Proceed."

Clipboard woman inspects my face and compares it to a photo on a long sheet of paper. I'm almost expecting her to examine my teeth, like I'm a horse waiting to be sold at market.

"Please turn and face the wall." She points to my left and I swivel awkwardly on my heels. A one dimensional facsimile of my capture is playing out on a flat screen. I am forced to watch as my fake crime is shown in full. This time, I notice the odd way I appear to be walking, my heels almost clicking together with every step. The detail on my shoes is also wrong, there's a golden tone to my hair that doesn't look familiar, its fakery obvious, but only to me. When the capture has finished I turn to Scrim again, hoping that she might somehow have realised this capture cannot be real, but her face is hard-set and grim.

"Kaida," she eventually says, grabbing the clipboard off the woman and then waving her aside, like an irritating fly, with a flick of her wrist. "It seems the security team have been watching you closely for the last two weeks, as you have been caught showing unusual interest in the door leading down to the sublevels." She reads over the notes quickly.

"It isn't true," I say, amazed at how false the accusations are.

Scrim cocks her head to one side and frowns again. "The capture you've just seen was taken on Saturday morning, it clearly shows that you let yourself into the archives with your aunt's security pass."

"It wasn't...it isn't...I mean, I didn't go anywhere near the archives." The words tumble out of me in a jumbled mess. "I never left the flat on Saturday," I add urgently, willing her to believe me. Or if not to believe me, then at least to bend the rules for the sake of a friendship that I hope is as solid as it's always appeared to be. "I sat in my pyjamas the whole morning, Yarena can tell you, when she came home I was—"

"I know this is very distressing,"Scrim interrupts me gently, placing a hand on my arm to calm me. "But it might be better if you just admit you

22

went down into the archives without permission."

"But it isn't true, I didn't!" I say with as much force as I can muster.

"You were caught on more than a dozen security captures."

"Then they were all faked too, I stayed in the flat the whole day." My voice is rising with the panic I'm beginning to feel again.

"But captures cannot be faked," Scrim says slowly and precisely, as if explaining some unbreakable law of physics to a slow-to-catch-on child. And that's when I know I'm beaten. Scrim must have heard this same pathetic plea of innocence hundreds of times before, from anyone hoping to avoid punishment for their crimes. I sound exactly like a criminal caught in the act. And if Scrim doesn't believe me, no one else will even give me a chance to explain. "I'm sorry, but the standard punishment for such a crime is two years at a juvenile detention centre," Scrim continues uneasily. "The capture alone is enough to convict you, no trial is necessary. There will be no question of you ever becoming a captologist."

The clipboard woman coughs quietly to attract our attention; she looks over her shoulder and nods at a man who suddenly emerges from the shadows at the far end of the room. He's tall and made from slabs of solid muscle, his nose is bent, his eyebrows abundant and surprisingly bushy for a man with such a degree of baldness. Scrim is almost as startled by his presence as I am. She tugs me by the sleeve, tucking me into the side of her body like I'm four years old, and she's trying to protect me from an angry barking dog.

"Tobias?" Scrim says, still sounding cool and in command but she's clearly rattled by his intrusion. "I don't recall inviting you into my office. To what do I owe the pleasure?"

"A short while ago, a thorough search of Hummingtree's home was conducted, and three captures were discovered hidden in her room," he says without preamble.

He places three sleek canisters on Scrim's desk for her to examine. The numbers on the sides match those that I supposedly stole. This is way beyond bad. Even I'm starting to wonder if I suffered some kind of blackout on Saturday. Maybe I did sneak down into the archives? Maybe the capture I've just experienced is real and I'm a genuine capture criminal, with a severe memory problem. The only thing I know for sure is there's now no way I'm making it out of this room with any kind of future.

"Thank you for bringing this to my attention, but this is a college matter, I can handle things from here," Scrim says, refusing to look at the canisters. She folds her arms instead, daring the man to outstay the welcome he never received. "You may go."

He stands his ground, his gaze shifting towards me in question. It's clear that this isn't the reaction he was expecting from Scrim, and that he'd like to witness my trial right here in her office, followed by my immediate incarceration. But instead of arguing with her he simply gives Scrim a surly looking nod, and strides towards the door without a backward glance, dragging his unspoken disapproval behind him. Scrim's eyes stay fixed upon him, but she offers no explanation for his sudden appearance, or how he might be involved in my strange capture tragedy.

As the door closes behind him it's like a trigger-pull. My chest begins to heave and I can feel I'm about to lose it with spectacular abandon. The clipboard woman backs away in utter disgust, and it's the judgemental look on her face that forces me to pull it back from the brink. I refuse to give her the satisfaction of being right about my breakdown threshold.

Scrim puts a reassuring arm around my shoulders.

"All is not yet lost," she says gently, lowering me into a chair like I've seen people do on those crime dramas, when someone's just been told that their husband/mother/dog has been murdered by a serial killer. "The police have given me a certain amount of discretion in matters of capture crime, for students who show promise," she says, allowing the words to sink in. "You're not the first person ever to get caught stealing from the archives." I think of the other detainees from the seats outside her office, and imagine a stealing spree brought on by exam stress, the cold weather or other equally unlikely causes. "Nobody wants to send a fifteen year old girl to a detention centre, Kaida, certainly not one with such an exciting future ahead of her, so I'm happy to say it's within my power to offer you an alternative."

I literally stop breathing. Alternative to the detention centre? If it involves counting rocks in a quarry I'll take it in the blink of an eye.

"If you agree to volunteer for a year, a place will be held for you on your course and you can take it up next December, without any blemish on your record. Nobody outside this room will ever know that you've been caught stealing from Cassian Cromwell, it will be as if it never happened. Do you understand what I'm offering you, Kaida?"

I manage one small nod. But the only thing I really understand is that this day just leapt from bad to catastrophic, in one heartless bound. Volunteering is the only alternative that could be any worse than the detention centre. Volunteers have some of the highest injury rates on the planet. Most end up with bits of their bodies crushed, mangled or missing, or with some kind of deep psychological or emotional trauma. A few end up dead. I, more than anyone, understand the truth of that. They get sent into the most hazardous captures, the ones that no sane person would ever agree to enter, such as those taken in the middle of war zones, hurricanes, or in remote mountain regions, where dangerous rockslides can wipe out several volunteers in one go, including my sister.

Detention centre or the risk of serious injury, it's not much of a choice. In fact detention centre would be the smart option. At least then I'd get to live out the rest of my life with all my limbs accounted for. I have no desire to become a legend before I'm sixteen. But Scrim is clearly keen to steer me firmly towards volunteering.

"We don't usually accept volunteers under the age of sixteen," she says, studying me for any warning signs of a meltdown. "But as far as the rest of the college is concerned, we will simply say that you volunteered to get a head start in the captology programme, that inspired by the bravery of your late sister, you wanted to jump straight into the action. You will have the instant admiration of every student here."

And their instant pity when I end up at the bottom of a collapsed mine shaft with a fractured skull.

"According to the protocol, I'm supposed to give you precisely thirty seconds to decide, if you refuse the offer, you will be taken directly to the detention centre in Clerkenwell, and Yarena will be informed of your conviction later today. But Kaida," Scrim pauses, making sure I'm braced for the gravity of what she's about to say, "I would urge you to volunteer, that way I can try to get to the truth of what's happened. If you accept your sentence at the detention centre, it will be viewed as an admission of guilt, and it will then be virtually impossible for me to make anyone listen to your accusations."

"So...you believe me, you believe my capture was faked?" I ask, way beyond feeling anything but the last shreds of hope.

"I don't know what to believe," she says. But she's looking me straight in the eye, which means she doesn't think I'm a total liar either. "All I can promise is to find the truth, whatever that might be. Now, I'm afraid I must have your decision," she adds uneasily, glancing at her watch.

Thirty seconds to decide on my future? If I had a whole week it still wouldn't be long enough. But there's no one here to plead my case, or my innocence. It's up to me. I've seen the detention centre in Clerkenwell on the news before, it's an airless, sunless, joyless facility. Those who are eventually released find it virtually impossible to land a good job, or to find a college that will accept them onto any course. Denied the right to live a normal life, they're often forced into a low paid, unskilled, poverty-trap existence. I'd rather take the danger, I realise, with an unexpectedly strong reaction in my gut. If injury comes, at least I'll be known as brave, strong, fearless. And if by some miracle I make it to the end of my volunteering year, with all my limbs in good working order...

"Okay." I nod once before I can analyze my reckless decision too deeply. "I'll volunteer."

Scrim sighs and squeezes my hand, relieved that she doesn't have to go to Yarena with the news of my shock detention. "Don't tell anyone about the faked capture until I've had a chance to investigate," she says, pulling me out of the chair and hugging me warmly. "If there is something going on, it would be unwise to make a big fuss about it now, and alert the perpetrators to our suspicions. Promise me that you will say nothing, not even to Yarena or your friends."

"I promise," I say, feeling dazed at the rapid turn of events. But at least I now have one of the most influential people at the Institute on my side, ready to fight my corner. That's got to count for something.

The woman with the notes takes over. She guides me to another door at the far side of the office, thrusting her clipboard and a pen into my hands. "Sign this."

I barely have time to read the words *Volunteering Agreement* at the top of a sheet of paper before she's tutting loudly, glancing at her watch. "You don't need to read it; it just says you agree to becoming a volunteer." Her compassion is overwhelming.

There are several paragraphs covering terms and conditions that I should read, but this is not the moment to argue. I sign the form with a spider's scrawl, she grabs the pen the instant I'm done and opens the door, giving me a helpful shove over the threshold. And all of a sudden I'm standing alone at the top of some concrete stairs. I hesitate, wondering what I'm supposed to do now, if I'm allowed to leave. Nobody in a badly fitting suit appears so I head slowly down the stairs, my legs feeling hopelessly weak and unstable. By the time I reach the bottom, I'm stumbling about like a newborn deer and I urgently need a bathroom. I lock myself in a cubicle, thankful that the room is empty so I can puke in peace. Then I sit on the closed toilet seat breathing hard, trying to regain some control of my spinning head before I attempt the rest of the short walk home. But I'm in no hurry to get there.

I've scarcely set foot inside the front door, when someone grabs my arm and steers me firmly into the living room at the front of the flat.

"What the hell were you thinking?" Yarena rarely loses her temper, but when she does, it's like watching a firework display, with an impressive selection of rockets and whiz-bangs. I slump onto the sofa and let her explode; it's easier than trying to stop the inevitable, because she has always been against me becoming a captologist, for obvious reasons. Since Millie's death, six years ago, she's done everything she can to change my mind, which is why she forced me down into the archives for a whole day. She's also taken me on a fact-finding mission to a bakery, due to my lifelong, sworn-in love of muffins, doughnuts and anything with sprinkles. I think she'd prefer me to choose a career sizing maraschino cherries for a Bakewell tart production line, than a life as a captologist. And now I'm fulfilling her worst case scenario, a volunteer, in danger of meeting the same tragic end as my sister, and I have no plausible explanation to soothe her fears. I can add thoughtless, heartless niece to my growing list of new identities, none of which I asked for. In the history of bad days anywhere, this is a stand out, gold medal, award-winning example.

"I've just had a message from Aldora Scrim's office saying you've volunteered." Her voice raises a whole octave in disbelief. She's dressed in her usual work clothes, a loose fitting white shirt and tailored black trousers, but her fine blond hair is showing definite signs of being grabbed and pulled by agitated hands. "Is it true?" she demands.

I take a deep breath and nod. Yarena flaps her arms in the air. "I don't believe it! What on earth possessed you? I thought you wanted to take sensible captures for those LoveNature people?"

"I still do, some day," I say quietly.

"Then how could you be so stupid? Especially after what happened to Millie, or have you conveniently forgotten about that? This is the most ridiculous decision you've ever made in your life. Was it Hekla's idea?"

It's such an absurd notion I almost snort. "Hekla doesn't even know yet."

"Did somebody force you into it then? Are you being bullied by one of the seniors at college?" There have been cases of bullying in the distant past, but the Institute has had a zero tolerance policy for a long time now, and bullies quickly get weeded out and dismissed.

"Kaida," Yarena says more gently, forcing herself to take a deep breath, "we can still put a stop to this before it gets anymore out of hand."

There's such a note of despair in her voice that I almost crack. I drop my gaze to the floor as I shake my head. "Nobody forced me, it was all my idea. I just wanted to be like Millie." The lie grates at my insides, but I've made a promise to Scrim, and if it's the only way to get to the truth...

I snatch up my bag and head towards my bedroom, before Yarena can hit me with another round of impossible to answer questions. "Can we talk about this later, I don't feel very well."

She shadows me all the way down the hall, shouting and yelling about the dire consequences of my thoughtless actions, the dangers of the life I've so recklessly chosen, how disappointed my parents would be if they were still alive, how much I'm behaving like an ungrateful, immature child. I shut my door and lean against it, listening as Yarena finally gives up and stomps back towards the living space with her unspent anger. I imagine sparks flying from the tips of her fingers, the last of the fireworks fizzling out, for now. I drop my bag on the floor, hoping to regain some sanity, but not even my own room is a safe haven any more.

A pile of clothes is sitting at the foot of my bed, clothes that don't belong to me, volunteer's clothes already delivered. Maybe by the same person who claims they searched my room and found three canisters? I glance around quickly, but there are no signs that anything has been disturbed, not even the dust on my chest of drawers, there's no evidence that anyone has done anything but place the clothes on my bed. I inspect the black trousers and top, instantly despising the slippery feel of the cool fabric and I hurl the whole pile into the corner of my room. Then I climb into bed and pull the covers over me, wondering how this day, which started with such an abundance of hope, could have ended with my whole future balancing on the sharpened blade of an unknown assassin.

4
McKenzie

I wake the next morning at 6.02 a.m. Measles is curled up at my feet, snoring gently, anchoring me to the bed and the life I lived before. I lay for several minutes wondering what would happen if I simply refused to leave my bed. Would Cooking Fat storm into my room with a handful of guards, who would lift me bodily from the sheets and then dress me like a doll?

I stroke Measles, shifting her gently to one side, and head for a hot shower, hoping the steam might relax the aching tightness that has settled in my chest overnight. I've also woken up with a new feeling, as if my brain has already started to come to terms with my unexpected status as a volunteer, leaving me with a quiet determination to stay whole and intact. It's the only way I'll ever find out who the man called Tobias really is, and why he's apparently trying to ruin my life.

I've never even considered the concept of enemies before. Apart from one minor disagreement with Erica Plimpton over a bicycle bell, when I was eight years old, I've never been on the wrong side of anyone. But someone has faked a capture, someone who clearly believes I don't deserve a future at this Institute. So whether I've done anything to deserve it or not, I now have at least one enemy in this world. And enemies, I'm quickly discovering, can be a powerful motivation.

My only other option is to pack up my most precious possessions and leave the Institute, my home, and everything else I know for the life of a runaway. But where would I go? Who could I trust to help me? A hat might disguise my silvery Hummingtree hair, but I'd have no real chance of evading all the facial recognition cameras and security drones that patrol the streets, day and night. And then a cosy room at the detention centre would quickly become my new home. For the second time in less than twenty-four hours, I realise I'd rather volunteer.

My new clothes fit perfectly, encasing my body in a thin but robust layer of flexible fabric. It has a slightly rough, sandpaper texture on the outside, for grip, and reflective strips on the arms and legs. The black shoes are lightweight with room for my toes to spread out to their natural shape. I stand next to the living tree in the corner of my room, pulling my sleeves all the way down to my wrists, where they snap tight against my skin, and study myself in the mirror. I look older, sturdier, not the same naive Kaida Hummingtree who left the flat yesterday morning. But I wonder if the stretchy material is truly strong enough to hold me together, if my new resolve fails and I have an epic meltdown. There are no pockets big enough for tissues. Maybe volunteers aren't supposed to cry?

I tie my hair back securing it with two pins; I always keep a small supply handy for hair and other emergencies. Then I glance at the open door of my wardrobe, wishing that Millie would step out of the shadows with an irritating grin on her face, and tell me how to get through this nightmare, because my boots will have to stay here, at home, where they can do nothing to help me.

When I finally slouch my way into the kitchen, Yarena has already made breakfast. The dark circles under her eyes proving that neither of us got very much sleep last night. She looks careworn, the morning light picking out the fine lines on her face and the creases in her forehead, that have deepened a good few millimetres since yesterday. I'm not really hungry but I sit at the table and eat three slices of toast with eggs, knowing that my body needs the energy to function properly. Yarena hovers and I can tell that yesterday's conversation concerning my life choices is about to rear its ugly head again.

"There's still time to change your mind, Kaida," she says softly, filling my usual mug with hot, cinnamon-scented milk, poured straight from the pan, a childhood favourite that she hasn't made for me in years. She's playing dirty, trying to remind me that I'm still young enough to enjoy such coddling, but I've got to stick to my decision. "One word from me and Aldora will tear up your volunteer's agreement," she adds, dangling the promise like an extra present on Christmas day. "You could be sitting in the cafeteria with Hekla by lunchtime, and we can forget this ever happened."

I'd like nothing better. Me and Hekla could make fun of the geeks, crowded around the LondonCall terminals, while working our way through a huge plate of cheesy chips. But it can't happen. It might never happen again. The sudden lump in my throat makes it impossible to swallow, and I have to spit a gob of masticated eggs onto my plate. The congealed yellow mass is the perfect metaphor for my state of mind.

"I've made my decision," I say quietly, concentrating on my milk, grateful that Scrim obviously hasn't mentioned the faked capture or the looming stint in a detention centre.

From the corner of my eye, I see Yarena nodding, as if this is the answer she was expecting. She sighs heavily and leaves the kitchen pulling her dressing gown tightly around her. She returns two minutes later with a worn pouch bag, which she places on the table in front of me with a little more force than necessary.

"You'll need this," she says. "It belonged to your sister, if you're going to be a volunteer, this might help keep you safe. Millie would have wanted you to have it."

I risk looking directly at her for the first time since my big announcement. It's hard to see the sadness in her face, knowing I'm the one who put it there. I stand up swiftly and give her a tight hug, breaking away before any tears can come and spoil my thin veneer of control.

"Well open it then," Yarena says, wiping her eyes with the back of her hand.

The pouch is leather made and has already seen an interesting life. All of its rips and tears have a story to tell, a story involving my sister. The thought gives me a small shot of passing courage that I try to hold onto. I run my fingers over the leather and undo the knotted tie; inside I find a compass, inscribed with Grandma Hummingtree's initials, *E.H.* It's old and scratched but has a good feel in my hand, and I love it instantly.

"Thanks," I say. "This is perfect."

At precisely 7.00 a.m., I somehow force myself to leave the flat. Cooking Fat is waiting outside the door, silent and surly looking, as if he'd rather be anywhere else. I don't need to ask where he's taking me; everyone knows the volunteers train down in the sublevels. The Long Walk is empty as I swipe through the door at the bottom of the stairs, and at this time of day no one is around to witness my tragic walk of doom. Cooking Fat uses his security pass to open the door that I supposedly snuck through on my capture-stealing crime spree. Anger is beginning to replace shock whenever I think about the unfairness of my situation, but there's no time to dwell on it now. We bypass the door to the archives and head down another level, down into the deep bedrock of London again, and a part of the Institute I've never seen before. Cooking Fat opens another security door with a brief nod at me. This is where his babysitting duties end; I'm on my own now. I can't say I'll miss his stimulating company; the plastic ducks in our bathroom have got more interesting things to say for themselves.

I head warily past a row of closed supply cupboards to my left and follow the sound of voices I can hear up ahead. The air in the sublevels is cold, fresher smelling than the archives but with a hint of something like explosives. More than twenty percent of all volunteers get injured in explosions in war zones and mines I remember, dredging up an almost forgotten statistic that I heard several months ago now.

I turn right at the end of the supply cupboards where the corridor opens out into a wider space; the stone walls, floor and ceiling give it the feeling of a tomb with a worrying lack of escape routes. A dozen people have already been marched down to the sublevels, several turn as I join the stragglers at the back of the group. I recognise the girl with the pink hair from outside Scrim's office, she's standing with a sullen expression, her arms tightly folded in defence. Most of the group are a good three years older than me, evenly split between boys and girls. One of the tallest boys has a shaved head, with a tattoo of a gorilla pounding its chest under his left ear. Two of the girls are already in tears, so it's clear that me and Pink Hair aren't the only ones who didn't have a choice about our new career paths. I'm beginning to wonder if faking captures is the only way the Institute can get enough volunteers.

For the first time I consider whether Millie might have been forced into volunteering too. I've been so wrapped up in my own fears for the last twenty-four hours, that it never occurred to me that she might have suffered the same fate. Up until the day she volunteered, she'd been planning her future life as an actress, spending long hours in her room, acting out scenes from her favourite films and plays, using me as an extra when peasants, onlookers or dead bodies were required. She was a natural extrovert, comfortable and content in the limelight, it made her glow with a quiet kind of happiness. I remember the furious fight that broke out when she came home one day in early August, and announced her sudden change of plans. Yarena yelled at her for hours, accusing Millie of volunteering so she could perform on a much bigger stage, where fame is guaranteed if the public takes a liking to you, and everyone loved Millie. Volunteers lead such dangerous, daredevil lives that some become as well known and idolized as any famous football player or movie star. So Millie Hummingtree, with her silvery hair and natural ease in front of any camera, became a firm favourite almost overnight. For a few short months, her face was on every magazine cover and gossip feed, every detail of her life followed, dissected and discussed. And I'd always assumed that was exactly what she wanted.

She moved into the volunteers' living quarters the day after the argument and I never saw her again. There were no visits or LondonCall conversations in the last four months of her life, so I never got a chance to ask her anything about volunteering, never got to say goodbye. Is it possible that she didn't choose that life, or death? Am I following in her fatal footsteps in more ways than one? The horrible thought makes my stomach churn, and I have to breathe deeply to settle the partially digested eggs, still swirling around my insides.

A sudden disturbance at the front edge of the group brings me back to the present, and I stand on the tips of my toes just in time to see a man calling for quiet.

"Listen up everyone, my name is Cyrus Roth, and I'll be your instructor for the next week." Silence falls and I squeeze through a gap behind Gorilla Boy to get a better view. Cyrus Roth is only slightly younger than Yarena, judging by the number of years showing on his face. His unshaven chin hints at a sprouting of ginger stubble. Large veins run down both sides of his neck, the kind that are always popping with rage in kid's animations, the deep gouges and scars on his hands don't inspire confidence.

"If you're expecting a welcome speech you've come to the wrong place," he says with an edge in his voice like a bag of rusty nails scraping together. "If you've volunteered to impress your friends and family, you've come to the wrong place. Each and every one of you has just made one of the worst decisions of your life." He lets those heart-warming words echo around the corridor until a much deeper, more troubled silence descends. "If you're standing before me now wondering how long you're going to stay in one piece, you might just make it through to the end of your year. A healthy fear of injury is one of the only defining characteristics of all volunteer survivors. You!" He points suddenly at Gorilla Boy who stands to attention like an army cadet. "Why did you volunteer?"

"Because no one else at my college had the guts to, sir," Gorilla Boy says with a certain swagger, even after everything Roth has just said.

Roth shakes his head in disapproval. "It's the idiots who think like you who get injured out before the end of their first assignment. The girl standing next to you!" Suddenly I'm in the spotlight and I feel my entire body convulse. Unlike Millie, I'd much rather live my life unnoticed, far away from the kind of attention she thrived on. "You'd better have a more intelligent reason for volunteering."

The whole group is now waiting for my answer; pressure builds inside my chest until I say the only thing I can. "I did it for my sister, Millie Hummingtree."

The name has a predictable effect on Roth, he hesitates, looking me over, weighing me up, but his expression gives nothing away. I concentrate on the veins in his neck, clinging to Millie's pouch bag, which is concealed inside a small pocket like a life raft. Several of my fellow volunteers mumble quietly to each other and I feel my face burning.

"Before you start your training, you'll need some basic supplies and equipment," Roth continues, silencing the group again. "Treat them with respect; these supplies might save your skin more than once."

Less than ten minutes in and Roth's already talking about loss of life. I swallow hard wondering if I'm about to break the record for the shortest time ever served as a volunteer.

We move off further down the corridor and I manage to dawdle until I'm at the back of the group, making it harder for anyone to stare at me. Roth leads us into a large storeroom area filled with the smell of boot polish and waxed canvas, where we line up and move past a tall counter that separates us from regimented rows of warehouse shelves and boxes. I collect a large army-green rucksack, like everyone else, and shuffle forward as it's filled by storeroom staff with gloves, boots, a waterproof jacket, lightweight tent and a survival pack with compass, flares, whistle, penknife and a flint and steel for lighting fires. There's also an emergency food pack containing dried fruit, two vacuum-packed meals with stringy looking chicken and bullet peas, three bars of energy cake stuffed full with seeds, nuts and desiccated coconut. Nobody makes any jokes; even Gorilla Boy has stopped grinning as the slow cogs in his brain turn over Roth's words about staying alive. A doctor in a white coat stands at the end of the line with a table full of syringes and small glass vials.

"Inoculations!" Roth shouts as we inch towards the table. "Everyone roll up the sleeve on your left arm, I said left!"

"What do we need inoculations for?" one of the older girls with long black braided hair whispers, looking warily at the needle. "Where the hell are they sending us?"

"There's a rumour going round that Scrim's decided to put us into one of the Death Valley captures, to see how long we last," Pink Hair says.

"I heard we're going to the Arctic to camp on an ice shelf," Gorilla Boy adds, still sounding cocky and undeterred, but he keeps his voice down so Roth can't hear.

I remember seeing a report about some volunteers that were set adrift in the middle of the Indian Ocean once, and I hope we're not destined for anything with deep water. The cold I could handle, maybe, but being marooned in a boat... I look away as the doctor sticks a needle into my upper arm, which instantly goes numb, the strange sensation travels all the way down to the tips of my fingers making them feel five times their normal size, which also makes the next task difficult. Roth shows us how to pack our new clothes and equipment properly into our backpacks, which doubles up as a seat, pillow and actual life raft if we ever get dumped in the sea, or swept away by a swollen river.

Then we move straight into another room for training, no time to obsess about any of the worrying things that have just happened. Roth is joined by several other staff members who each look like ex-army or special ops forces, with the scars and facial tics to prove it. A short woman is the scariest, half her head has been shaved revealing an elaborate inked-in picture of a claw, but even that cannot hide the alarming dents in her skull. She stares down anyone who even glances in her direction like a demonic bulldog.

We split up into groups of three and I'm with Pink Hair and a boy with blue eyes. There's something vaguely familiar about him. Maybe he was at my old school? Or maybe his family lives at the Institute too and I've seen him in one of the big public capture booths?

Bulldog Woman shows us the basics of map reading, using an Ordinance Survey map of Scotland as an example of terrain. Then she throws in a compass and begins to demonstrate how to tell north from south, and the perils of confusing east with west. I let my attention wander for a few moments as I already have a good idea about maps and compasses. I learnt from Grandma Hummingtree when we used to stay with her and Grandpa in the summer months, at their wild, magical, sprawling farm in Northumberland. I'd trail behind Grandma as she meandered through the old barns and outbuildings, then we'd walk together on the beach, collecting driftwood for a fire, sheltering from the wind behind the sand dunes as we toasted marshmallows over the blue salted flames. My favourite part of the whole day was listening to the stories she told about when she was young, and totally obsessed with captures, and how she hiked all the way to London on foot, just to visit the booths at the Institute. I've always wondered if she's the reason I'm obsessed with captures too, did I inherit her capture-loving nature? Maybe I'm the only Hummingtree who was ever really destined to be a volunteer? I'm not sure I'll ever discover the answer to that question now.

I thank all the stars in the wide Northumberland sky that during those splendid days at the farm, Grandma Hummingtree taught me how to navigate my way across mountain ranges, moors and dense woodlands. It takes time for that kind of knowledge to sink in, which means I've got one survival tool in my pocket already.

I risk a quick glance around the room as Bulldog Woman shows Blue Eyes how to hold a compass correctly. The rest of the groups are tackling fire lighting, shelter building and something to do with taking notes that I can't quite fathom. When it's my turn to use the compass, I don't let on that I understand how it works. Nobody likes a know-it-all and I've already attracted enough attention to myself as Millie Hummingtree's sister. So I make deliberate mistakes, dropping the compass ineptly, drawing an irritated head shake from Pink Hair. The boy makes notes about everything in a small hard-backed book. I accidentally catch his eye when he looks up and I'm struck by his expression. Everyone else in our group is angry, traumatised or overly eager due to a lack of working brain cells. But Blue Eyes seems focused, serious, single-minded, he's soaking it all up like a deep-sea sponge, keeping it locked away for his own reasons. But it's impossible to tell what those reasons are.

I'm still trying to remember how I know his face when it suddenly hits me like a stomach punch. His name is Wren McKenzie. His brother, Kit, was a volunteer at the same time as Millie. And it was Kit's fault that my sister died.

No one outside the Institute has ever witnessed the whole tragic incident, even though it's standard practice to take a capture within a capture, whenever a group of volunteers goes on any assignment. Barely ten shaky seconds of capture was ever released by the Institute, showing the rockslide that killed my sister. But what it did reveal was Kit McKenzie, in a desperate scramble to save his own skin, pushing Millie out of his way as she tripped and stumbled behind him. Kit McKenzie died too, further into the same assignment, but not even that fact can erase his guilt. And the whole world has blamed him for what happened to my sister ever since. His family bore the brunt of that hatred and a silent demarcation line was drawn. Even though they lived two floors below us, even though Kit's parents still worked in the administration department at the Institute, none of my family ever acknowledged their existence again. And now I am sitting just inches away from Kit's youngest brother.

I feel my face flush with hatred, or maybe I'm angry at being forced into such close proximity, angry that he's here to witness my fear. The similarities between the two brothers are so striking, that I can only put my slowness to recognise Wren down to the advanced state of fear I've been living in since yesterday. The fact that we're both now volunteering together has such an eerie echo of the past that I shudder, and try to edge away from him. Wren McKenzie. I've barely given his existence a thought in years. I've seen him less than half a dozen times at the Institute, our paths crossing only in crowded corridors or noisy cafes, where it was easy to avoid any direct contact. But his presence is now burning a hole through my side, like I've been struck by hot coals leaping from a newly woken furnace.

I glance at him swiftly. One look is enough to know that he is fully aware of who I am. The lack of shock on his face suggests he's known for some time, and has already adjusted to the idea, because instead of trying to pretend that he doesn't exist, or avoiding my gaze with shame and embarrassment, he's staring at me with obvious curiosity. I turn my back on him. Wren McKenzie is one extra problem I definitely don't need right now.

I do a sly evaluation of his appearance a few minutes later, as Bulldog Woman shows Pink Hair how to concertina a map. He's stocky but not a muscle-head like Gorilla Boy, his hands are strong and nimble, he's got a thick mop of tufty blond hair that looks like it's been hacked into shape with a pair of garden shears, and his eyes are the cornflower-blue of summer. A large number of volunteers that I've seen on the news look like different versions of Gorilla Boy, all brute force and naked ambition. You can tell that if they make it through their year in good shape, they'll go on to become glorified, overpaid, celebrity security guards, or something else requiring very little brain power. Me and Wren both stand out for our age and our wide-eyed, rabbit-in-the-headlights appearance. Neither of us really belongs here. But it's deeply uncomfortable sharing *any* common ground with *this* boy. And I'm not sure how much more bad news I can handle in one week.

When we move onto fire lighting, I have to play dumb again. Thanks to Grandma Hummingtree, I could build a blaze with a flint and steel in a force nine gale, with a bucket of water being poured over my head. It's almost funny watching Pink Hair trying to ignite some mossy twigs, Wren is even more hopeless, but he sticks with it, showing a streak of determination until he finally succeeds. Lunch is a meat stew with dumplings, which we all eat together sitting in a big circle on our backpacks, with all the awkwardness of strangers. I move as far away from Wren as possible and sit next to Braided Hair, before anyone else realises who he is, and why us being here together is so bizarre and potentially sensational. Gorilla Boy – whose nickname is actually Rilla – holds court, telling everyone how good he is at building fires. He fills the silence easily until Bulldog Woman shouts at him to shut up. I grip the inside of my new shoes with my toes, missing the familiar dips and ridges that my feet have worn into my old boots. And I wish I was sitting at home with them right now, safely tucked away in the dark of my cupboard, where they're waiting for my return like a faithful dog.

Shelter building is uncomfortable and irritating. Me, Wren and Pink Hair work together for the first time, with Pink Hair taking control as the oldest, so there's no need for me to speak. Under her command, we manage to construct a lopsided disaster using ferns, a tarpaulin and some sticks. It collapses on top of us as soon as we crawl inside. Pink Hair blames me for tying the tarp to the wrong sticks, and Wren for not following instructions properly. But all three of us know the real reason it crumpled so quickly — because Pink Hair understands shelter building about as well as most people understand the molecular formula for capturing a moment in time. Pink Hair and Rilla would make a dream team.

Our last rotation of the day is the basics of data recording, which up until now I'd never known to be a survival skill. But Bulldog Woman gives it just as much weight as all the other things we've learned, drumming it into us that this is crucial, that when it is required, we need to record data clearly, concisely and accurately. We learn how to pack glass vials into a padded bag so they won't break if we trip and fall. We learn how to use GPS trackers and laser beams for taking measurements and recording exact locations. And I start to wonder if the rumours are true, and Scrim is sending us on a Death Valley walk for our first assignment.

When Roth tells us we're done for the day, Pink Hair pushes me aside as she storms out of the training room. We're definitely not destined to be lifelong friends, even if that life turns out to be distressingly short. Wren deliberately waits until I file through the door, letting me put some distance between us. I can't wait to leave the dark oppression of the sublevels. When we reach the Long Walk and we're suddenly free again, everyone dissipates rapidly. I practically run for the far end, dragging my backpack along behind me, ignoring the curious glances of people I push past. When I reach the flat it's empty. Yarena is still at work, she spends so many hours in the archives sometimes that when I was little, I used to wonder if she was allergic to sunlight or fresh air. But I'm glad she's not home right now, because I know exactly what I'm going to do, and she would definitely frown on the idea.

I drop my backpack, rip off my black uniform and fling it to the floor. The only reason I don't trample it to death is because I've got to wear it again tomorrow, and I don't think Bulldog Woman would approve of the dusty-shoe pattern I'd love to cover it with. I find my favourite blue jumper, pull on my most comfortable jeans and warmest socks and slowly lace up my trusty boots, starting to feel like an overly anxious version of my old self again. I grab a cheese sandwich from the kitchen and scribble a note for Yarena, so she won't panic when she comes home and finds the flat empty. Measles has to be fed and stroked before I finally take my coat, hat and scarf and head for Yarena's office at the top of the hall, right next to the front door.

I breathe in the familiar, reassuring smell of freshly sharpened pencils and open reams of paper. Yarena's living tree is neatly decorated with painted antique eggs in blue, green and gold. But the only thing I'm really interested in is the door at the far side. Behind it, a set of narrow wooden stairs leads straight up to our own personal capture booth on the roof, a small toughened glass box, a fraction of the size of the one I used in college. In these early booths, some of the first ever built, the landscape of the capture rolls beneath your feet along with a special floor, like a treadmill, which allows you to roam for miles without ever reaching the edge of the booth, assuming it doesn't get stuck or break down first. The newer booths have a more reliable, high-tech gyroscopic system, synched perfectly with the capture, but I still prefer the feel of our ancient glass box. There's a patched hole in the roof, the floor has collapsed in one corner and is littered with leaves and twigs. I love the slightly mouldy smell, the rippled glass walls and the old-friend-buzz I feel just from standing inside it, even when it's empty and unused.

And I'm not here to use it now. I head straight for the emergency exit door on the far side and push through, making sure it closes properly behind me. And then I'm standing outside, two hundred feet above the pavement below.

5
The Lid

I've never been the daredevil of my family; that title would have been awarded to my mum, who used to do stilt walking for fun, or Grandma Hummingtree, all-round adventuress. And this thin metal-grid walkway that I'm now standing on, the one that hangs precariously over the edge of the building, hundreds of feet above Cromwell Street, the one that creaks and groans in the wind like it's complaining about the cold, has always scared me to death. I creep along, clinging to the railing with both hands, remembering the time that Millie forced me out here when I was seven years old, and I had a screaming fit. But it runs past all the booths on this level and it's the quickest way to reach the rooftop garden. It would take thirty minutes using a more convoluted route through the Institute, and thirty minutes is too long.

I inch my way past the next booth, which belongs to our neighbours, the Zimmermans. At this time of day it's empty, Mr. and Mrs Zimmerman both work in the administration offices. But the booth beyond theirs is definitely in use, I can see the light from a capture bouncing around inside so I walk as silently as possible, even though I know the occupants will be oblivious to my presence. Then I stop at the edge of a rusting hole in the metal walkway. It's an easy jump to the other side; a child of eight could cross it without any difficulty. But I hesitate, leaning warily, staring down at Cromwell Street a very long way below, scared to death that my foot will somehow slip and I'll drop like a stone, that I'll have enough time on the way down to see all the life that I haven't yet lived, flashing before my eyes. It takes another minute before I've worked up enough courage to step across it. I climb over the locked gate at the end of the walkway and it's a short drop down into the garden, which spans the entire length and width of the building. My feet are happy to be back on solid ground.

The Cromwell Institute was one of the first buildings in the capital to create a large scale rooftop garden, which eventually led to The Greening of London. Now every new building has to be a minimum of forty percent green, meaning the roof space and some of the walls are usually covered in trees, grasses, trailing plants and sedums. This ensures that every inner-city resident can see an abundance of living things, and breathe the same clean air as the ivy and the birds nesting inside it. My favourite green buildings are the Irving Tower, which has a spectacular arboretum on the roof where maples, cedars and oaks form shaded woodland walks. And the Bronte Museum of Books, where tumbling honeysuckle cascades down the outside like a waterfall of frothy green. The garden at the Institute is a mirror of the Royal Parks that still exist at ground level London, with a boating lake and gentle slopes of lawn, ideal for cloud spotting in the lazy heat of summer. Today, the sky is already edging towards darkness and the air is cold enough for hoarfrost to form, but I enjoy the harsh sting of winter on my face after being stuck in the sublevels all day.

I follow a well-worn path through a gathering of oak trees, where me and Millie used to come on windy days, so we could listen to the giants creaking. Then I hurry on towards the welcoming lights of the gondola station, which connects the Institute to the city below. I join a queue of people already heading for home, catching the first gondola which stops at Mole Valley. Its real name is Lower Level Clapham, but everyone calls it Mole Valley as it's one of the largest subterranean areas of the capital, and that's where Hekla lives. After the strangest, most frightening forty-eight hours of my life, I desperately need to see a friendly face. Yarena's way too upset and angry to offer the kind of company I need right now. Hekla's the only person who will understand, without me having to explain every feeling and thought inside my head.

I keep my hat pulled well down over my ears, to hide the silver of my hair, and find a seat in the corner as the old-fashioned wooden gondola carriage swings clear of the roof. It glides silently over the stately buildings of historic London, and for the first time since the capture booth in college, I can breathe freely again. I settle into the ride, trying to concentrate on my immediate surroundings and nothing else. The first gondola station we stop at is for Westminster Bridge. From this height, I can see an early evening crowd of people, wandering through the friendly shops and restaurants that line the bridge on either side. Then we're riding high over the Thames, silty-looking and dreary in the winter dusk, clogged with river taxis and a flotilla of floating homes that move with the tide, like a brightly coloured waterborne circus.

On the other side of the river, the gondola glides slowly downwards, entering a gaping concrete hole in the ground, which is ringed with bands of steel. This is the gateway to the subterranean levels. Our descent is pitch-black and tortoise-slow, and I stare at the friendly yellow glow of the carriage lamps until we reach the station at Mole Valley. I leave the carriage and take the first exit that brings me out onto the main street.

This is London mark two, an underground city constructed when there was no space left above ground to build on. Concrete pillars take the place of trees, lining the streets and stretching all the way up to The Lid, the colossal slab of bedrock that marks the boundary between the two cities. Above The Lid sits London with St. Paul's Cathedral, the Houses of Parliament and Buckingham Palace. Below The Lid, the Mole Valley housing projects, high-rise blocks of flats, parks, cinemas, shopping centres and everything else a city needs to function. Sunlight is mostly artificial, but those few areas where toughened-glass roof panels reveal the world a long way above ground, have become as exclusive as Mayfair and Chelsea, and way beyond the means of most Molers.

I follow the road heading east, keeping my eyes fixed firmly on the shop windows, which are filled with neon lights and garish displays to compensate for the dullness, looking at anything but The Lid above me. Claustrophobia is a major problem in the subterranean levels. Starved of natural sunlight, many Molers have also developed eye problems, mental health issues and soft bones. It's like the sky has already fallen in. I hate the way each sound echoes around me like a trapped animal searching for an escape route. If I had to live here, I'd go crazy in less than a month.

Hekla lives off the High Street on Gaskell Road, which is one of the most crowded and narrow, but I've come this far so I'm not turning back now. I take the lift to the tenth floor of Hekla's building, a grey concrete box, and hammer on the front door of number one hundred. As usual, it's the nosiest flat on the entire floor, with several clashing strains of music pounding against the outer walls, which vibrate with the volume, threatening to crumble to dust. Hekla eventually answers the door.

"I've told you ten times already, Gideon, turn that music down!" she yells over her shoulder. She's dressed in sunshine-yellow jeans, purple T-shirt and bare feet with toenails painted the same red as her patent leather boots. "I'm sick of listening to those same brainless songs, over and over!

It sounds like a troll chucking rocks at a dustbin!"

When she finally turns to face me her eyebrows jack upwards in surprise. She grabs my hand and drags me inside, leading me up to her room without saying a word. I've always liked Hekla's home precisely because it's so different to the quiet and calm of my own. She lives with her geologist mum, computer-tech dad and two older brothers who are both at university. A tight-knit family, they pretend to get on each other's nerves, but they're always fiercely protective and loyal. Gideon waves as we pass his open door and he cranks up his troll music just to annoy Hekla. She slams her own door in response, but it's surprisingly quiet inside the room, with only the distant thump of a beat now leaching through the walls.

"Where in the name of Cassian Cromwell have you been?" she demands, facial muscles strained with concern. "I've left tonnes of messages on LondonCall, I've been round to your flat three times, but there's never anyone at home. I even asked Mr. Reese the college administrator about you, but he's totally bonkers, he just kept telling me that you've left the course!"

I sit on the edge of Hekla's bed and remove my boots. Her room is covered in discarded clothes, odd shoes, antique computer screens, every drawer is open and spilling its guts out onto the floor, with a kaleidoscopic clashing of colours. Her bed is a crumpled nest of tangled sheets and blankets, her living tree died two years ago, suffocated by a pair of knotted socks that eventually severed the roots. But right now, this room is the safest place on earth, or under the earth to be exact. And I'm so relieved to see Hekla I can suddenly feel a torrent of emotion threatening to slide down my face. But I can't lose it yet. I need to get everything off my chest and out into the open before it crushes something inside me.

"Mr. Reese was telling the truth," I say, yanking back an overwhelming urge to blub. "I have left the course."

Hekla's mouth curls into a smile. "Are you serious?" She's expecting a joke to follow and then some harebrained explanation for my absence.

I nod. "I'm deadly serious." Which is true in more ways than one.

Hekla's whole body is motionless, her open mouth gaping wide, like a rockfish feeding on plankton, as she tries to decide if I'm still working on a joke. So I try to describe everything that's happened, from the moment I stepped into the capture booth at college, to the end of my first day as a volunteer. I'm breaking my promise to Scrim but I know Hekla will never repeat a word of it. She lets me talk without interruption, the smile slowly fading as she realises there's nothing funny about my tale. It's much harder than I thought it would be to tell her the incredible story, because saying everything out loud for the first time removes it from the nightmare realm, and dumps it straight in the middle of my horrible new reality. When I finally pause, Hekla slumps onto the bed beside me, putting an arm around my shoulders to show her solidarity.

"So basically, I'm now the only person, apart from Scrim, who knows you're not some crazy, thrill-seeking, pain-in-the-arse volunteer?"

I grin. It feels foreign and the muscles in my cheeks protest. They've been set, pinched and scowling, for the last two days.

"And you're also telling me that you're only on the volunteer programme in the first place, because someone faked a capture with you in it?"she questions.

"Yeah, but I don't know if Scrim really believed me, and then someone called Tobias turned up with the canisters I supposedly stole. It was either this or two years in a Clarkenwell detention centre."

Hekla shakes her head before rising to her feet again. She begins to carve a path through the debris on her carpet, pacing while she digests everything I've told her.

"This is really serious, Little Dragon."

Little Dragon is Hekla's pet name for me, ever since she discovered it's the literal translation of my name, chosen by my mum after a holiday to Japan. I can't help smiling. My whole world has been knocked sideways and tumbled upside down, but to Hekla, I'm still just Little Dragon. We have always been a strangely suited pair. Hekla was named after a volcano in Iceland, or according to Hekla, the volcano was named after her, so we both come from fire. Since the day she discovered that my parents were dead, she's been looking out for me like the older sister I lost a few years later. With such a shocking lack of family, I'm not complaining, it gives me a true sense of belonging. And I've slowly been assimilated into the landscape of her family, my presence expected at all their celebrations and gatherings. I don't need to ask if she believes my story either. I know she accepts it as the truth, without question, even though it sounds like a bad script for a B-grade movie.

"So the question is what do we do now?" Hekla says, still pacing, pulling her blond hair back into a ponytail, a sure sign that she's doing some serious thinking. "Obviously we have to find out who this Tobias bloke is, and if he faked your capture. I mean, why would anyone do this to you?"

I shrug my shoulders. "Maybe it's the only way the Institute can get enough volunteers?"

"So why not pick on some nerdy nobody from Mole Valley? Why choose you? Everyone's heard of your sister, so the fact that you're now a volunteer too will be internet-breaking news when it gets out," Hekla says. "Plus someone's gone to a lot of trouble, convincing the security team that you've been lurking around the entrance to the sublevels. There's something really seismic going on, something unbelievably weird."

"You mean besides the fact that someone actually faked a capture?"

Hekla stops, stunned again by this fact, even on a second hearing, and she stares at me with wide eyes. "I can't even think about that little nugget without food."

I follow her down to the kitchen, say hello to her dad, who is working on his laptop at the table, and then we raid the fridge. Hekla grabs a tray and piles it high with cold chicken curry and rice, chocolate orange ice cream and cheese straws. We carry the supplies up to her room where we clear a space on the floor and sit, working our way through the food mountain. I'm surprisingly hungry and I eat two helpings of curry before diving into the ice cream. The food has a calming effect and I can feel myself unwinding just a fraction. I lean back against Hekla's bed, toes digging into the carpet, one hand holding onto my boots. Hekla hoovers up the last snacks and then sits, cross-legged, elbows resting on her knees, studying me closely.

"Loads of people have tried to fake captures in the past, but if anyone had done it, I would have heard, it's like the big banana, the Moley Grail." Hekla's knowledge of capture news and developments is almost equal to that of any qualified technician, who already works at the Institute. She reads every tech journal in existence, spending hours online, trading gossip and information with her large group of techie friends. Then she squirrels it all away in her brain, like she's part computer herself.

"If this was the work of a rogue tech-head, they'd be bragging about it all over the internet. So it's got to be an inside job, someone at the Institute has done this and managed to keep their mouth shut."

"And if someone at the Institute *is* faking captures, mine's probably not the only one. Some of the other volunteers definitely didn't look thrilled about being there, and they got called into Scrim's office too," I say, wondering if the boy with the mono-brow is now locked inside the detention centre.

"Do you reckon Scrim's behind it all?"

I shake my head. "She nearly had a heart attack when she saw me in her office, and she looked even more shocked when that Tobias bloke turned up with the canisters. But she couldn't bend the rules just for me."

"So maybe this Tobias is working with some lunatic technician down in the sublevels," Hekla suggests. "I've heard some of them go crazy after working underground for so many hours every day."

"That's why I'm always telling you to get outside more."

"It's already too late for me," Hekla grins, clamping a hand over her forehead in mock despair. "I'm just one long computer session away from completely frying my motherboard."

It's a relief to joke about things, but it feels even more alien than smiling, and the light heartedness fizzles out quickly. We both understand how serious this is, but it's easier to skirt around the edges of the black hole we've stumbled upon, than to dive straight into the abyss.

Hekla leaps up suddenly and grabs her favourite laptop, which she keeps in a bright red patent-leather case to match her boots.

"Time to brush up on my hacking skills," she says, flexing her fingers as she sits opposite me on the carpet again, and starts attacking the keyboard with frightening confidence. When it comes to computers, I know nothing but the basics, how to surf, how to message on LondonCall, how to upload pictures and videos. But Hekla understands computers like neurosurgeons understand the wiring of a brain. She can dive straight into the circuits, plunge into the inner language and pluck out extraordinary pieces of information that most people wouldn't even know existed.

"I'm bringing up the Institute's own network," she says concentrating, her agile fingers typing speedily. "If I can access the student records, I might be able to find out where the faked capture came from at least."

"You can do that without anyone noticing?" I ask, surprised.

"How do you think I always know my own exam results before anyone else?" Hekla raises an eyebrow at me with a look of pure mischief. "It's not because I know any brilliant psychics."

I sit and absorb the news that my best friend is an old hand at hacking. But I shouldn't be surprised. Hekla's interpretation of right and wrong has always been more *advanced* than most people's.

"Right, I'm into the student records. That was a lot easier than it should have been for an Institute with the world's most advanced technology," Hekla says, grinning from ear to ear, buzzing with the thrill of her conquest. "Do you want to hear what they said about my interview for a place on the technician's course?"

I scramble across the carpet on my hands and knees and bunch up beside her, shoulder to shoulder, so I can see the screen. The display shows a picture of Hekla along with a list of exam results and personal information. At the bottom is an assessment from her interviewer.

"'McKellor seems to have an impressive grasp of computing and technology,'" I say, reading it out aloud. "'Her intelligence quotient score is in the highest percentage of any age group, so I have no choice but to recommend her for a place on this course. But she displays a total disregard for authority that could be problematic in the future.'"

Hekla's smile widens. "The interview guy was a twerp; he kept picking his nose right in front of me and expecting me not to notice, so I might have been a bit sarcastic."

Hekla's sarcasm is legendary, finely crafted from years of sparring with her older brothers, and known to scold anyone unlucky enough to be in the firing line.

"So, let's see what your record says, Miss Goody-Two-Shoes."

I feel an unpleasant tug behind my belly button. What if my student record is as full of lies as the faked capture? What if Hekla starts to doubt that I'm telling the truth? That would be worse than anything else that has happened so far. To have my best friend look at me like I'm a liar. But it's too late to stop Hekla now. She's already typing my name into the search box, scrolling through the results she picks out *Kaida Hummingtree*.

"That's weird, I can't get in," she says, frowning at her screen. "The record's locked, it won't open without extra security codes, and I can't access those either."

I know it's irrational but I'm almost relieved.

"I don't suppose Yarena still knows anyone in the tech labs that could help us, from the days when your dad worked there?"

I shake my head. "She's never mentioned anyone and I haven't got a clue who Dad worked with. Yarena says he didn't talk about it much."

"That's because all techies have to sign a confidentiality agreement. I'll try again later," Hekla says, and I can literally see more hacking plans forming inside her brain.

I glance at my watch, it's getting late and I don't want to worry Yarena even more than I already have. I grab my boots, tie my laces and clamber to my feet, hauling Hekla up beside me. But there's one last bombshell I need to drop on her.

"One of the other volunteers is Wren McKenzie," I say, pulling on my hat and coat, waiting for her reaction.

She trips over a pile of unwashed T-shirts and twists back to face me. "Seriously? Wren McKenzie, that weedy kid with the blond hair and the no-good dead brother?"

"He looks just like Kit, but he's not weedy or a kid anymore," I say picturing Wren's all too familiar features. "I've got no idea why he volunteered, but it's like we're repeating history or something creepy."

"Well, I'd bet my best red boots betrayal runs in his family, so just stay out of his way, okay?" Hekla says, making me promise. "I'll find out everything I can about your new friend Tobias, and if he's a psychopath, I'll let you know."

"Thanks," I say, winding my scarf around my neck. "It's always good to know who the psychopaths are."

"And don't get yourself injured in the meantime." Hekla's voice is light and breezy but I know she's just as worried as I am about the dangers that lie ahead of me. "I'll have no one to drag along to the Earl's Court Tech Show in the summer, if you get sucked into a giant whirlpool."

"I'll try not to ruin your plans," I say following her slowly down the stairs. I suddenly feel very reluctant to leave and my feet stick to the floor like they've been freshly dipped in tar. If I hid out at Hekla's, how long would it take Scrim and the others to track me down? Could I live under The Lid for the rest of my days, a wretched fugitive, concealed in an airless attic cupboard with only mice and cobwebs for company, to avoid the fate I do not deserve?

It's only a fear of ending up in the detention centre as a volunteer deserter that keeps me walking, because even an attic cupboard sounds like an appealing idea right now.

6
Booth Number Ten

The next week is given over to training. I spend eight hours a day in the gloom of the sublevels, feeling like a nocturnal animal, because by the time I make it back up to the flat again it's already dark outside. And I don't see the daylight once.

In the training room, we revisit the fire lighting, shelter building, map reading, data gathering and record keeping skills. In all the news reports and special documentaries I've ever seen about volunteers, nobody ever mentioned all this paperwork. The other volunteers think it's strange too, we were all expecting something a bit more action-packed and dangerous. Rilla struggles with the sheer amount of notes we're required to take and instructions we're expected to remember. Thinking really isn't his strong point.

"Why aren't we doing any training captures?" he complains more than once, when Cyrus Roth steps out of earshot. "What use is a stupid clipboard going to be if we get cornered on a cliff edge, by a pack of hyenas, and have to parachute into a gorge?"

He and Pink Hair have formed a friendship based on their mutual love of complaining about everything. Some of the other volunteers, including Braided Hair and a boy I call Raven, because his dark glittering eyes remind me of a bird, have also paired up or formed small groups at lunchtime. But nobody has made any effort to speak more than a few words to me. After some initial curiosity about my sister they quickly lost interest. I'm so much younger than most of the volunteers that I'm easy to ignore, which suits me well. I prefer my own company. Trying to make conversation with a bunch of people I have nothing in common with, except for our current confinement in the training rooms, is my definition of torture. Wren is the only person who sits near me, but I maintain a strict regime of stony silence and refusing to meet his eye. It's clear that he'd like to talk but I won't give him the satisfaction. What am I supposed to say to Kit McKenzie's brother? It's not like we can chat about the weather, or trade funny capture stories, even if I wanted to, which I definitely don't. I wonder if his persistent closeness is a pathetic attempt to make the other volunteers hate him a little less, because Wren has been picked on mercilessly, since our second day, when Raven suddenly realised who he was. And his every move around the training room is now followed by the constant hiss of threats and insults.

"Just wait until we get sent into some deep caves or ravines," is one of Rilla's favourite taunts. "Then you'll get what's coming to you, Sparrow Boy."

Wren never rises to the bait. He doesn't try to defend himself or his brother by returning the insults, his silence is stoic. But I see his fists ball into white knuckles a dozen times a day; I watch the angry creep of red as it inches up his neck and the tightening of his lips into a thin steel band, so I know he's not as calm as he's pretending to be. And I wish he'd sit somewhere else, study someone else when he thinks I can't see him watching me. I have enough to occupy my thoughts without trying to fathom out his strange motivations. If he's hoping I'll forgive his brother, he's misjudged my character badly.

On the Friday morning, I arrive at the sublevels and it's obvious that this day is going to be different. There's a whole host of people I don't recognise, busily arranging rows of lights and hiding microphones, and I realise it's the day of the volunteers' official welcome.

This happens every year. Cassian Cromwell shakes hands with the latest batch of volunteers, thanking them for their service, complimenting them on their bravery, throwing them into the spotlight. The whole spectacle is broadcast live but I never thought I'd be part of it. The idea that my face will soon appear on every phone, computer and TV screen in the country is so alarming, that it's all I can do to keep my breakfast from making a comeback. What will people say when they see the small, inexperienced sister of Millie Hummingtree, already looking way out of her depth and scared to death? Comparisons to my sister will begin all over again, but I can save everyone the trouble. Millie was twice the person I will ever be, brighter, funnier, smarter by far. And I don't even feel sour about it. Especially now I have serious doubts that she ever wanted the life she ended up living.

Roth keeps us all well out of the way while the production team set the stage, moving lights into position, putting up gold reflectors so we all look healthy, glowing and keen. It's all part of the show, and from this side of the camera it looks totally fake. Some of the volunteers are already angling to make an impression. Rilla, Blond Spikes and Pink Hair are mixing with the crew, cracking jokes, being helpful, so when it comes to time on camera, they will get more than their fair share of the limelight. Wren is the only other member of our group who shrinks away from all the fuss. He isn't in this for the fame. But the production crew have got other plans. This is their big moment, when they can reveal to the world that me and Wren are both volunteers, and they stand us side by side at the end of a line, ready for the drama that will undoubtedly draw the biggest audience in years. I feel even more nauseous thinking about the unwanted attention I'm about to get.

When the production team are finally satisfied with their arrangements, we're told to stand on our own individual marks, don't fidget, don't squint into the lights, no smirking, laughing, whispering or pointing, speak only when spoken to. I suspect there are less stringent rules about meeting with royalty. Roth gives us a last minute pep talk about not embarrassing ourselves, or him. And then suddenly we're on air. A presenter woman, with stiff lacquered hair and an irritating nasally voice, is saying a short piece to camera about what an inspiring group we are, how fearless and strong. And then she turns to greet a small cluster of people who have joined us in the sublevels. Aldora Scrim leads the way beaming gracefully, the other members of the board all tag along behind looking a lot more animated and friendly than the last time I saw them in her office.

It's the sight of such two-faced audacity that flips the switch inside my head, and I suddenly know what I'm going to do. The idea is so pure and crazy that it's a freedom just to consider it. When Cassian Cromwell shakes my hand, I'm going to tell him, and the rest of the country, about the faked capture that brought me here. With the eyes of the nation fixed firmly on us both, nobody will be able to sweep it under the carpet; the truth will be out in the open protecting me from any fallout, from being bundled off to a detention centre. Exposure will save me. At the very least, someone will decide I've had a total breakdown and send me to hospital for an assessment, but anything is preferable to the fate that awaits me in volunteer land. If Scrim's not certain she can save me, I'll have to save myself.

"You look like you're going to be sick," Wren whispers beside me, as Scrim and her group meet with the first volunteers, the cameras following their every move. "Your skin's gone all pale and clammy."

"Don't talk to me!" I say angrily, earning myself a warning glare from Roth, who stands just off to one side, like a sheepdog keeping its flock pinned inside a pen.

"I'm just saying, if you're going to hurl, maybe you could direct it away from me," Wren whispers as Cassian Cromwell finally makes his grand entrance. "I don't want to meet Cassian Cromwell for the first time smelling like vomit."

All the cameras turn to catch this most auspicious moment. Cassian Cromwell's mere presence transforms the occasion into something extraordinary, one of the most famous and powerful people in the world, and he's heading straight towards us with his trail of stardust.

I dig my nails into my palms, trying to work up the courage to carry out my harebrained plan. If my voice comes out in a squeak, I'm doomed, if Scrim gets to me first and sees the crazed look in my eyes, she'll steer Cassian Cromwell away from me without a second thought. The last thing she wants is a sensational freak-out drama for the whole world to see.

I take a long, slow, deep breath. Wren shifts away from me slightly, misinterpreting the signals. Scrim is talking to Rilla who grins and waves cheekily at the camera, hogging all the attention like a pro. As the group moves down the line, I can feel the heat of the lights building, adding to the pressure of the moment, but I manage to hold it together. I clear my throat quietly, ready to deliver my unrehearsed bombshell and that's when Scrim looks directly at me, suddenly sensing trouble ahead. She turns her back towards me, halting Cassian's progress and changing his route, so that they travel back up the line towards Pink Hair. Scrim ignores the frantic signals coming from the production team, who've been saving me and Wren for their dramatic finale, and the moment is lost. Just seconds later, Cassian is being guided away and the glare of the lights finally dims.

Everyone's talking loudly over the top of each other, repeating what Cassian said, the way he made a joke about Rilla's tattoo. I lean back against the wall, deflated. My one chance to tell Cassian Cromwell what's really happening at his beloved Institute, and I blew it by clearing my throat. Scrim didn't want a scene. Or maybe she wanted to avoid the revelation that I'm supposedly a thief, the sister of Millie Hummingtree, a huge disappointment and potential jailbird. That definitely wouldn't look good.

There's no time to dwell on my dismal failure, because Roth is suddenly herding us together and yelling at everyone to shut up.

"Now that you're all famous, it's time to get down to some real work," he says, checking his watch. "In precisely thirty minutes, you will enter your first capture assignment as volunteers." This news creates an even bigger buzz than Cassian Cromwell but all I feel is a fresh wave of nausea. It's a lot for one poor gut to cope with in a single day. And then someone else is heading down the corridor towards us. I recognise him instantly.

"Hey, that's Tobias Troy," Rilla says in hushed, awed tones to the rat-faced boy standing beside him. "He's one of the toughest volunteer team leaders the Institute's ever had."

He's also my sworn enemy, the man who produced the damning canisters in Scrim's office. Just the sight of him is enough to double my sky-high levels of anxiety and my palms begin to sweat profusely.

"Troy once made a group of volunteers crawl through quicksand, just to see how many of them would survive," Rilla says quietly.

"You're so full of it, Rilla," Rat Face whispers. "That's just a dumb story made up to frighten new volunteers."

"It's the truth, I swear on my tattoo! And anyone who refuses to carry out his orders gets sent to a back-to-basics training camp, in the Australian Outback."

Troy is dressed in the same military-style clothes as Cyrus Roth and it's obvious, even before he speaks, that he doesn't possess Roth's limited people skills. He surveys us with a scowl, like we're a group of snot-covered, back-chatting delinquents he's just been ordered to babysit.

"This is Tobias Troy, your team leader," Roth says, greeting him with a single nod. Rilla nudges Rat Face and they both gawp at Troy in open admiration. "He will be taking you through your first capture. Listen to his instructions and follow them to the letter, and you might just make it through the rest of the day in one piece. Remember your training, keep your wits about you, and try not to behave like a bunch of lunatics."

Troy catches my eye and then looks away swiftly. If he's planning to confront me about the canisters supposedly found in my room, or my presence on the volunteer programme, he's saving it for later.

"We'll be heading into capture booth number ten," Troy says in a deep voice that has obviously been strengthened by a lifetime of yelling.

A more subdued murmur travels through the group. Everyone's heard of booth number ten. It's one of four extra-large booths, each the size of three football pitches laid end to end, which means the potential distance we can roam inside any one of them is vast, hundreds of miles. A wide chasm has been excavated beneath each one to allow for ravines, caves and deep ocean beds. Long before I was born, one of these booths was set aside each Christmas for a special festive capture, ice skating on the frozen Thames, a replica Victorian market complete with roasting chestnuts, gas lamps and horse-drawn carriage rides. Or a forest of Christmas trees decorated with colourful fairy lights and paper lanterns, pine sap so fresh you could feel the stickiness on your shoes for days afterwards. But I don't think we're heading for Santa's grotto.

These four booths are now used exclusively by some of the most experienced volunteers, who enter them to explore other planets, or dangerous crime scenes, as the crime is being committed, or to study violent natural events, like the calving of an iceberg as it falls off the end of a glacier. Each booth is ringed with metres of reinforced concrete and steel, anchored in bedrock, and nothing has ever punched through these extra layers of protection. Any capture, no matter how violent, can be contained. So everyone knows that if we're being sent into booth number ten, we're heading for trouble.

Troy leads us beyond the training room we've become so familiar with, and down to the very end of the stone corridor, which is sealed with a large steel door. He opens it with a swipe card and hurries us through into a chamber on the other side, where four more reinforced doors have been set deep into the wall, like gateways to another realm. Troy dives straight into booth number ten. Inside there's an enormous changing room, tall enough and wide enough to house any vehicle or digging equipment, even a helicopter with its blades already turning could sit comfortably in this cavernous, echoing space. He points to a pile of equipment that's been dumped next to a row of benches and lockers.

"Stow your backpacks in those lockers, they won't be needed today. Then everyone must put on a protective suit," he says, indicating a rail filled with dull, silvery coloured, all-in-one garments that look like they've been worn many times before. "And grab a gas mask."

"Hey, maybe we really are going to Mars," Rilla says, trying to hide the slight wobble of nerves in his voice with an extra show of bravado.

"Mars needs proper space suits with an oxygen supply, you idiot," Braided Hair says. "My cousin wears something like this when he goes down into London's sewers, to clean out the fat bergs."

"I'm not going down into any sewers," says Pink Hair, as she yanks one of the suits off its hanger and studies it distastefully. "It's not safe with all those rats."

"Some of the rats are already up here," Wren says quietly, brushing past me.

I take a suit and hold it up for inspection. It's been singed in several places and there's a clumsily repaired hole, the size of my fist, just above the left knee. Both the elbows have been stained by something yellow and the whole thing reeks of sulphur, like the last person to wear it has been rolled around in a barrel full of rotten eggs. The smell almost makes me gag.

I tie my hair back, securing it with two pins from my pocket, and try not to touch any of the stains as I pull the suit on. When everyone is finally ready, with toughened leather boots tightly laced, Troy helps each one of us into a large black gas mask with clear bug-eyes. He saves me for last, letting me stew in a cauldron of my own nerves and jitters, then he pulls the straps in tightly so the mask seals against my skin. His eyes linger on my silvery Hummingtree hair with the kind of malevolence that only a sworn enemy can summon up at such short notice. And I'm grateful for the protection of the gas mask, which apparently stops skin from withering on the bone.

"Take a worksheet before we go inside," Troy says, handing them out from a thick pile. We've been training with similar worksheets all week, but this one is more like a book. It's fifty pages long with boxes to tick and questions to answer, although it's impossible to tell what those questions relate to. Next we're given GPS trackers, pockets full of glass vials, and a roll of small metal hammers and chisels in different sizes. They look like something an untrained travelling dentist might keep hidden in the boot of their car. I wonder if we're heading for a contaminated false teeth factory, or a frontline hospital in a war-torn country?

I glance around nervously at the rest of the group. For once, Wren doesn't try to catch my eye. Pink Hair is visibly shaking; everyone else is standing silently, waiting for our next instructions. This is the moment when we truly become volunteers, whatever hazards and dangers we're about to face there will be no emergency exit buttons or rescue teams. Volunteers live or die by their own quick thinking and bravery. If it turns out that I haven't got enough of either, my career will be a short one, my name added to the very long list of those who have already been injured out and broken to the core. I feel for the compass in my pocket and hold it tightly, trying not to hyperventilate inside my gas mask.

Less than a minute later, Troy leads the way towards a heavy-duty air locked door that seals the entrance to the capture booth itself. The screen above the door, the one that usually gives details of temperature, terrain and special conditions is blank again, but the green light above it is already on.

"Single file entry," Troy yells, making sure he's got everyone's attention. He's wearing his own silvered suit but hasn't bothered with the gas mask. "Wait for my instructions, do not go wandering off by yourselves, this is not a trip to the beach, and there will be no building of sandcastles."

Without another word he opens the door and heads inside, beckoning Rilla to follow. All I can see is a cloud of swirling mist, but the smell of sulphur is overpowering and it's clear my mask isn't completely airtight. I shuffle forward as volunteers disappear, one by one, past the point of no return and I'm suddenly inside the booth. I can instantly sense that the space we've entered is vast, that this has more in common with a mighty cathedral than with the tightly packed college booths up on the third floor. Someone seals the air locked door behind me; the noise vibrates through my body like a warning shot fired from a cannon.

The first thing I do is check that I'm standing on solid ground. The surface beneath my feet is made of blackened rock, and even through my boots I can feel how jagged and tough it is. The rest of the group are already clustered around Troy and I join them quickly, just as the mist clears and I can finally see what lies beyond. And I know that this is where I'm going to die.

7
Dead Weight

We're standing on a crater rim, staring two hundred feet straight down into a gigantic open sore in the ground, filled with boiling lava. For our first ever capture assignment as volunteers, we've been sent into an active volcano. And we're clinging to the edge like chicken wings waiting to be chargrilled. If Troy's doing this to see who's got the guts to carry on, I'll hand him my guts right now, if he'll just let me leave. I don't even care if he thinks I'm a coward, cowards live longer.

"Your task today is to complete the questions on these worksheets!" Troy shouts, trying to focus our attention on the job at hand, like it's just another day in the training room. But his words are drowned out by the loud hiss of gases being vented around our feet, a dragon's breath of evil smells and dangers.

He points to our destination, a wide ledge halfway down the crater. I swear I see him smile, just for a second, like he's feeding off our fear, and I wonder if Rilla's story about Troy and the quicksand has some grain of truth after all.

Troy strides over the edge into the crater and the sheer scale of it is dizzying, a vast angry hole the size of a lake. There's no path so it's slow going down the uneven surface that tries to trap our feet in narrow fissures, and trip us up with jagged rocky spurs. My heart is pounding like a jackhammer inside my suit, partly because it's bone-meltingly hot, and partly because I'm petrified of sliding down to the very bottom of the crater, where the pool of lava churns and rages like an inferno. I've never experienced such naked fear before, no amount of training could have prepared me for how vulnerable I feel, how difficult it is to stop myself from cowering, from using Rilla as a human shield. Humiliation is almost a price worth paying for such protection. Somehow, I manage to hold it together and keep control of all my bodily functions, but it's a close call. This is the most insane thing I've ever done. Even my sister never hiked down into a volcano. But the molten fire is also mesmerizing, it's impossible not to stare into the lava, which looks capable of vaporising whole buildings, an entire fleet of army trucks or bulldozers would be melted down and liquefied in seconds, nothing on earth could withstand such an intense heat for long.

It takes twenty minutes to reach the ledge, and the noise of the volcano has intensified into such a roaring presence that it wipes out all thoughts, all fears, all communications between the different parts of my brain, until all I can do is stare.

"Collect the samples, answer each question, do not take off your gas masks, do not touch anything with bare hands. Work as quickly as possible, you have two hours!"

No one moves. We're all as petrified as the rock we stand on, wondering if this is some kind of sick joke. Wren is the first to venture out further onto the ledge, breaking the spell, and then we all begin to fan out cautiously, straying no more than ten feet from the rest of the group, staying well away from the edge. The old saying 'there's safety in numbers' has never felt more real than at this moment, and I hope there's some meagre protection in it. I move clumsily in my suit, stumbling on the uneven ground. Lava fields stretch into the distance as far as I can see, forming the steep sloping sides of the volcano, a black alien-looking landscape where no plants have dared to grow.

The heat is so intense, even through the protective silvered suit that I feel like a turkey being roasted at Christmas. Sweat pours from every part of my body, pooling horribly in the creases of my neck, the crooks of my elbows and behind my clammy knees.

I find a spot as far away from the edge as it's possible to get and begin to take samples, scraping, clawing, chiselling bits of the volcano away and sealing them inside glass tubes, neatly labelled, boxes ticked, questions answered, exact locations given using my handheld GPS locator. All the training we've done makes the task almost bearable in the surroundings, but everyone is rushing, fumbling in their gloves, racing through the questions with a life or death sense of urgency. It's while I'm scraping some rock into a glass vial that I start to wonder what we're even doing here. In the very early days of capture history, volcanoes were explored so thoroughly that there's nothing new left to find. We know everything it's possible to know about lava and magma, and about why and when eruptions occur. So why do we need more samples now? It doesn't make any sense.

I get hotter and hotter inside my suit until I think I'm going to pass out. I put all the samples I collect into an insulated box that is way more protected against the heat than any of us volunteers.

"Everyone take cover, now!" Troy suddenly yells.

I join the crush of bodies as everyone rushes towards the back wall of the ledge, ducking down behind a large boulder, only turning to look when I'm safely wedged in tight. Boiling lava spews high above the ledge in a mini eruption, fountains of furious fire tumble over and over each other and then fall across the ledge where we've just been working, a warning that we're literally playing with fire. There's a sudden scream to my right. I turn automatically; it's Rilla, scrambling to his feet, holding his arm stiffly away from his body. And even from this distance I can see the smouldering patch on his suit, where he's been hit by a stray fleck of lava. Troy races over, pulling him back behind the rocks but Rilla's still yelling in a panic, attempting to rip off his suit. I close my eyes, trying not to imagine how it feels to have super-heated lava burning through any part of my body. Rilla's screams are getting louder and the lava shower continues to fall around us, but Troy's got to do something. He shouts at Pink Hair to take Rilla back up to the crater rim and out of the capture for urgent medical treatment. Rilla and Pink Hair hobble together, tripping and skidding their way up the steep slope; every single volunteer watches until they disappear over the ridge.

The lava shower subsides a few minutes later and Troy orders us to finish our worksheets as quickly as possible, but nobody moves. The ledge is now covered in searing hot lava pools, and none of us are willing to venture out into the newly formed landscape, nobody wants to be the next victim. Troy eventually has to winkle us out from behind the rocks, dragging us to our feet. Wren is the only one who goes voluntarily but his expression is grim. I dodge carefully between the puddles of lava, making sure no part of my boots accidentally makes contact with the glowing substance. It looks alive somehow as it cools and changes and slithers.

I resume my sample-taking duties, completing the questions on the worksheet with trembling fingers, so it takes twice as long as it should do. Time stalls until every minute feels like the longest ever recorded. It's impossible not to turn and stare at the lava, a fierce, unpredictable beast just waiting to leap as soon as my back is turned. But despite my out of control levels of fear, I'm one of the first to finish. Troy sends me to the back of the ledge to wait and I stand, mesmerized by the endless burning fury of the volcano. Wren joins me a few minutes later; the fingertips of his left glove are singed and blackened. He shakes his head but says nothing. When more than half of us have finished, Troy approaches the group with his hands on his hips and I can feel it in my heat-softened bones that this isn't going to be good news.

"I need one volunteer to take samples from a ledge lower down."

Troy's clearly been saving this little surprise until he's got some of the quickest sample takers to choose from. We all glance warily at each other wondering if anyone is stupid enough to raise their hand.

"I need one volunteer!" Troy repeats. "None of us is going anywhere until the entire assignment has been completed!"

No one moves, no one makes eye contact with Troy in case he takes it as a sign of consent. But I have a growing dread that he's about to choose me.

"You!" He points to Wren instead and I feel a small stab under my ribs. Wren hesitates then steps forward. Troy hands him a mercifully thin worksheet and a fresh batch of glass vials. Wren stows them away in his pockets and then follows Troy as he heads towards the lip of the ledge. I tag along behind with the other volunteers stumbling in my wake, driven by the disbelief that anyone, however unpopular and disliked, is actually being sent closer to the very heart of the volcano.

Troy is pointing at a steep slope in the far right-hand corner that appears to lead down onto a much smaller, narrower ledge of rock. Wren glances back at the group without focusing on anyone before he begins his descent. It's impossible to look away as he slips and clambers downwards, with no safety ropes or rescue plan. And I know he must be overriding every basic human instinct he possesses now screaming at him to turn tail and flee. I wonder how many of the other volunteers would have refused to go, would have taken any punishment, or jail sentence, over the alternative. If Troy had picked me, would I have been as brave as Wren McKenzie?

He's only halfway down the rocks when another violent lava flare occurs. This time the molten fire leaps and cascades towards us and everyone scatters, running for cover so quickly that Wren is instantly

61

forgotten. Only Troy and I stand our ground. We watch as Wren loses his footing and stumbles, trying to avoid a stream of lava that flows over the rocks just feet in front of him. He freefalls the rest of the way down to the ledge like a circus acrobat, with a cartwheel of silver-suited limbs, hitting his head hard as he reaches the bottom. Hot lava falls onto the rocks around him but he's lifeless and still, no flicker of awareness, no sense of the danger he's now tumbled into. I turn urgently towards Troy, expecting him to rally the others, to organise a human chain or a makeshift stretcher. But all he does is shake his head, he turns his back on Wren and starts to move away. I catch his arm and tug him back, but it's like trying to shift a mountain.

"We've got to help him!" I yell, determined to get a reaction.

Troy removes my hand from his sleeve like it's something dirty and disgusting. "If I send three more volunteers down to bring him back, chances are I'll lose all of them."

"But you can't just leave him there, he'll die!" I holler.

"He knew the risks when he volunteered," Troy shouts in my face. "Anyway, why do you care, Hummingtree? You of all people should be glad to see him suffer!"

Troy's right; this would be poetic justice. If I let Kit McKenzie's brother die it would somehow be an even reckoning, his life for the life of my sister. And I know that nobody would even blame me, or accuse me of abandoning Wren. But I can't do it. I can't just leave him there, sworn enemy or not.

I start towards the slope, hoping I'm not too late, that Wren isn't already dead or beyond help. I feel volcanic like anger at myself for possessing such a ridiculous code of behaviour, for risking my own life to save his. Troy yells, threatening me with all kinds of hazardous solo capture assignments in the lonely Atacama Desert, in the depths of the Mariana Trench and the active minefields of Angola if I don't turn back. But he makes no real attempt to stop me, and I realise he's just as scared as everyone else of losing his life in this fiery hell-hole of a capture.

As soon as I start down the slope the heat intensifies, the soles of my boots quickly become tacky and then begin to dissolve, leaving a melted-toffee rubber trail behind me. The noise from the crater is now deafening, it takes all my concentration just to keep my footing, but I finally make it down to the ledge. It's a tiny shelf, in danger of being totally engulfed, and

I realise my chances of making it back to safety are much slimmer than I'd calculated. But my body is now pumped so full of adrenaline that I can practically feel it dragging my blood through my veins, at an accelerated rate, and I know I cannot leave this capture without Wren. It could have been me lying here, unconscious, perilously close to the end of life. I have to believe that someone would have rescued me too.

I hurry over to Wren and kneel beside him. There's no response when I yell his name or shake his arm, not even the tiniest flicker of an eyelid. So I struggle to my feet again, slip my hands under his armpits and heave. Dead weight is unbelievably heavy and hard to move. It's as if Wren's body is deliberately gripping the ground I'm trying to move it across, and I feel every muscle in my own body complaining after only ten short steps back towards the slope.

I stop, change my grip slightly to get a better hold and drag him again, inch by inch, laborious and slow, totally out of step with the fury of the earth fire burning right beside me. It sounds like a mythical dragon or an evil spirit brewing up a death spell.

By the time we reach the base of the slope the rush of foolhardiness that has kept me going is almost spent. Even allowing for super-human strength in moments of extreme danger, I've barely got enough energy left to get myself back to safety. I sit on the hard ground breathing heavily, with Wren lying at my feet. My thoughts are hopelessly blown to bits by fear and exertion, so I do the only thing that feels right and rip off my gas mask. At least now I can think without sweat rolling down my face and into my eyes. The sudden heat on my skin is intense, it prickles like fire-threaded needles, but some of the panic subsides. I remove Wren's mask next, struggling to get it off without jarring his neck, but I can see his face properly now. I'm surprised at how young and peaceful he looks; wherever his subconscious has taken him it's clearly more encouraging than our current surroundings.

"Wren!" I tap his face as I shout close to his ear. "Wake up! I need your help or we're both going to die!"

His eyelids flicker. I'm finally getting through to him, but I haven't got time to take it gently.

"Wren!" I scream, slapping his face hard with the whole palm of my left hand until he flinches. I shake his shoulders, his head flops from one side to the other, like a nodding-dog on the dashboard of a car. When he opens his eyes, his pupils are unfocused, he's groggy and confused. But I haul him up to his feet, now that he's got at least some control over where he's putting them, and push him up the slope ahead of me. Then I rest his arm around my shoulders and half carry, half drag him the rest of the way, as he finally starts to register the seriousness of our situation.

Troy has organised the other volunteers into a rescue party, and as soon as we reach the upper ledge, Wren is hurried away from danger. Troy is careful not to meet my eye and we all trudge back up to the crater rim, leaving the lava and the heat behind us at last. I'm so grateful to be alive that I feel an intense mix of joy and trauma both fighting for space inside me.

When we finally emerge into the safety of the changing room, a medical team is already waiting to treat Wren. They help him onto a stretcher and wheel him quickly out of booth number ten, leaving the rest of us behind in a dishevelled, shocked and lightly steaming state.

Troy hovers, incandescent with rage as we change out of the sulphur smelling suits, and retrieve our backpacks from their lockers. He gives us a long lecture about how badly we've performed, what a disgrace we are to the name of volunteer, how ashamed he is to be our team leader. He then issues dire threats about what will happen to each of us if we don't show some improvement in our next capture. He finally dismisses the group who hurry away swiftly, before anyone catches the forked tail of his anger. I intend to follow, to head straight up to the rooftop garden and fill my lungs with clean fresh air, to chase any lingering volcanic fumes away. But Troy grabs my arm and holds me back until everyone else has fled, and we're standing alone in the changing room.

"You're coming with me, Hummingtree," he says, fingers digging painfully into my skin. "And you'll keep your mouth shut and your questions to yourself. I've already had enough of your backchat to last a lifetime."

8
Family History

For a horrible moment, I think he's about to force me back into the capture booth, to deliver some kind of quicksand punishment for disobeying his orders. But he hurries towards the stairs instead and then all the way up to the second floor of the college, still gripping my arm like he thinks I'm a flight risk. At this time of day, the corridors are deserted; every student has either gone home or is hunkered down in the library with a stack of books and a deadline. And I'm glad. I don't want anyone to see me being dragged along like a naughty child.

Troy swipes through a door and pushes me ahead of him into a long featureless corridor, finally letting go of my arm. The drab white walls and grey linoleum floors seem at odds with the grandeur in the rest of the building. He turns right and stops outside a room, number fifty-five.

"This will be your living accommodation from now on; you will sleep, breathe and wash in this block until the end of your time as a volunteer. Considering your age, Principal Scrim wanted to let you live with your aunt as long as it didn't cause any problems. But your behaviour today constitutes a big problem, Hummingtree." He towers over me, trying to intimidate, to reassert his authority. He will never forgive me for rescuing Wren, or for exposing a mile-wide streak of coward that runs through his nature, like a marbling of fat through a side of beef. And this is my punishment.

"I don't care who you are or what family you come from," he closes in so I can feel his hot breath on my skin, "disobey my orders again, Hummingtree, and you will find yourself being volunteered for every hazardous assignment going. What's one more volunteer casualty? It's not like there's anybody left to cry over you."

He drops a hefty set of keys and swipe cards at my feet and marches away without looking back. Several older volunteers wander past, watching the scene with curiosity. I let myself into the room and dump my backpack on a hard chair, swiftly locking the door behind me. I rub my aching arm, trying to bring some of the feeling back. Troy's fingers have left deep indentations in the skin, like I've been cattle branded. I could file a complaint against him. I've got the evidence right here on my body that proves he's using unnecessary physical force in my training. But I have a feeling it would only make things worse, so I study the room instead, trying to calm down.

Two duffle bags sit on the floor along with a box of bits from my bedroom. Clearly the decision to move me to the volunteers' accommodation was taken before today's capture. Yarena has gathered up all the things she thinks I might need or want; my bedside lamp, my elephant-shaped alarm clock and a perfect crystal for hanging in the window. I discover she's also hidden a cake tin at the bottom of the box, containing my favourite cupcakes, with extra sprinkles on top. I can't help smiling even in my volcano-weary state. I know this is her way of telling me to stay safe, even though she's still mad at me for volunteering.

The room itself isn't a bad size with one window looking out over London, and one single bed with a plain grey duvet cover. The walls and floor are the colour of charcoal, not a shade I usually favour, but I find the monotone scheme strangely comforting. Maybe it's because of the day I've just spent staring into boiling fires of lava, or the fact that my mood is as dark as my new surroundings. Or maybe some research scientists have discovered that charcoal is the perfect colour for keeping volunteers in a calm and unquestioning state, like throwing a blanket over the cage of a parakeet to stop it from squawking. Either way, I strip off, dump my clothes on the floor and take an extra long shower in the equally dark bathroom, letting the hot water ease the knots in my shoulders and the aching muscles in my legs, after dragging Wren away from the jaws of death. I wonder briefly if his injuries are serious enough to exclude him from our next capture assignment. Or to get him thrown off the volunteer programme altogether. Lucky him if they are. There's nothing he can do to change what's already happened, but at least his volcano days would be over before they'd properly started.

I dress in warm socks, a big slouchy jumper and comfy jeans, and unpack the rest of my belongings so my new room's a little less prison-like, a little more home-sweet-home. Then I sit on the deep window ledge, knees tucked up to my chest, and realise just how much I've been relying on my real home, on the reassuring presence of Yarena and Measles, the familiar routines and home-cooked meals, to keep me on the right side of stable. But I'm now more alone than I've ever been in my life. I'm also shaking badly, I notice, watching a tremor in my hands with mild interest, like my hands belong to somebody else. The rest of my body feels strangely numb like it's only my hands that grasp just how close I came to a lava-filled grave. My first capture as a volunteer and I was almost vaporized. I can't even explain my own actions to myself. Whatever logic I had for saving Wren, I'm relieved I don't have to justify my reckless rescue mission to Yarena. Maybe Troy has done me a favour after all? But he's also singled me out as a troublemaker, which makes my goal of staying intact for the next year, of finding out why someone faked my solo capture, twice as hard to reach. I'll have to melt into the background as much as possible from now on.

I wince at my own use of the word *melt*. After today, it will never have the same, harmless meaning again.

I hug my knees for a long hour until the heat under my skin begins to cool and my hands stop shaking. I decide food can't make me feel any worse, so I leave my charcoal box and head up to the cafeteria which stays open well into the night. I load up on chicken, potatoes, broccoli and a huge helping of jam roly-poly with custard. I need to keep my body fuelled. I eat alone, the cafeteria is virtually empty and I'm in no mood for company anyway, but I miss my boots. My toes are desperate for something to grip and the trainers I'm wearing are far too soft and spongy to give me any sense of relief or solace. When I've finished, I retreat back to my new bedroom feeling relieved that I don't meet any of my fellow volunteers on the way. I lock the door and try to settle into my new existence.

I sleep badly in the unfamiliar bed, woken by every unknown noise and stray light that sweeps under my door. At breakfast, I sit close to the other volunteers, listening in on their conversations. Most of the talk centres around a proposed trip to visit Rilla at the hospital, and whether they should take him a bunch of bananas, instead of a bunch of grapes, on account of his nickname. I also learn, after some mean sideways glances, that Troy has 'let it slip' that he sent me down to rescue Wren, that it was all his idea, not mine, and that I only agreed to go when he threatened to tell everyone I was a coward. It's such a huge lie it's almost funny, and I can't wait to tell Hekla how my story has been rewritten, how I am now the cowardly villain. Pink Hair and Rat Face then lead a loud discussion about how disappointed my parents would have been to have such a runt in the family, after the legend that was my sister.

By the time Troy rounds us up twenty minutes later, and takes us down to the sublevels again, I've earned my first volunteer nickname, Yellabell, short for Yellow Belly. A week ago, the fact that I've now been branded a coward would have reduced me to tears and caused some major anxiety, but I'm surprised to discover it doesn't faze me at all. I'm far more concerned about making it through another day without mortal injury. It's even more of a surprise to find Wren already waiting outside the booths. Half his head has been shaved down to the pink of his scalp and covered in short strips of bandage, which somehow makes him look as vulnerable as a chick that's fallen out of the nest, way too soon to survive. He ignores all the curious glances and whispers from the rest of the group, keeping his eyes firmly fixed on the ground. Apart from the pink scalp he appears to be uninjured and I feel something like relief. At least my rescue efforts weren't in vain.

Troy calls for silence and we all turn to face him. There's no sign of Cyrus Roth or any of the other training staff, which means we're heading straight for assignment number two, I realise, my breakfast threatening to rise up again.

"Today you'll be working in booth number eleven," Troy informs us coolly, like he's just announced nothing more dangerous than a morning of boot cleaning.

"So we're not going back into the volcano, sir?" Pink Hair cuts across him with obvious relief.

"As I was just about to explain," Troy frowns and she shrinks away from him, "we'll be working inside a different capture and this assignment will run over the course of two days, which means an overnight stay."

Somehow I don't think we'll be checking into a five star hotel and dining on steak and fries.

We enter the changing room which is cold and deserted. A pile of equipment waits for us over by the air locked door. We each take several packs of extra food, a mosquito net, and a tube of heavy-duty insect repellent, and stuff them into our backpacks. Wherever we're going, we won't be meeting any polar bears. I check that Grandma Hummingtree's compass is still sitting safely inside my pocket; it already feels like a lucky talisman. I need it now more than ever to protect me from whatever's on the other side of the air locked door, and from myself. This time, I'm determined not to play the hero, no matter what happens I'm keeping my finer instincts buried deep beneath my fear, where they belong.

I take a last look around the changing room and try to visualise how inviting and wonderful this dreary space will feel, if we ever make it back from the next capture.

Troy opens the air locked door and starts ordering everyone into a blast of heat coming from the other side, but this heat is totally different from the furnace of the volcano. This air seems thicker somehow, filled with unfamiliar earthy scents, it feels humid and sticky. The sun is burning hot but its strength is diffused by a canopy of immensely tall trees way above, and I crane my neck to see where they meet the sky.

"It's a nine mile hike to our campsite," Troy says. I hear the air locked door being sealed behind me. I already hate the finality of the sound. "There will be no worksheets today, but pay close attention to your surroundings. The rainforest hides many hazards and I won't be carrying any of you if you trip and break an ankle. Yellabell, you bring up the rear if you think you can handle that without messing up."

Pink Hair sniggers behind her hand and nudges Braided Hair, pleased that Troy has adopted my new nickname. But I'm happy to stay as far away from Troy as possible at the back of the group. We begin our trek slowly, finding our feet, settling into a pace everyone can manage. For the first hour, I put all worries about where this capture is leading aside, and try to take in my surroundings instead. The first thing that strikes me is just how beautiful the rainforest is, lush with green foliage and exotic flowers, their colours so primal and bold they barely look real. Luxuriant ferns cover the forest floor like a green ocean, resisting as we wade through the undergrowth, rippling like waves in the breeze. Long slants of sunlight pierce the canopy above, illuminating different sections of the forest, drawing my attention better than any spotlight. I've never been anywhere like it, not even in my school trip captures. The soft pattering of raindrops as they fall on fat leaves is surprisingly soothing, mixed with the rhythmic noises made by insects and calling birds, it sounds almost musical. Somewhere off to the right I can hear the roar of a huge river as it falls and tumbles over rocks, but its course is hidden by the trees. It's exactly the kind of capture I imagined myself taking sometime in the future, only I don't know if that day will ever arrive now, or if I want it to. Being volunteered has muddied the already cloudy waters.

"I didn't get a chance to thank you for saving my life."

Wren suddenly drops back from the rest of the group and walks in step beside me, as if continuing a conversation we've already started. He looks guarded, uncertain, but he has an air of determination also. "If you hadn't come down to the ledge to help me..."

His voice cracks and breaks, but the rest of the sentence is unnecessary. We both know how close we came to death by incineration. I can't blame him for feeling traumatized; it's a natural, healthy response to being in the presence of an active volcano. But I'm pleased he's clearly dismissed Troy's version of events, the one where I'm the coward. For some reason it seems to matter.

"I didn't want your death on my conscience," I say with a prickly tone, shifting my backpack so it sits more comfortably as I walk.

"Nobody else was troubled by their conscience," Wren says quietly, indicating the other volunteers ahead of us as they push their way through the thickening foliage.

I have no idea how to handle this conversation. But I also know I can't avoid it, and there's a part of me that wants to hear Wren talk, that admires his bravery and the way he takes all the insults thrown at him without ever lashing out. Although I sense I may have taken his place now as the most hated volunteer.

We walk in silence for several minutes. This is the closest we've ever stood to each other, apart from yesterday. It's hard not to notice his striking blue eyes, and the easy graceful way he walks, he has none of the awkwardness that makes my limbs trip and stumble under pressure. His hair is thick and springy with a mind of its own, and he doesn't seem to care about the peculiar shapes it forms. But he constantly brushes his right eyebrow with his left thumb, maybe it's a nervous tic, or maybe his brow feels as scratchy and irritating as a sock full of fleas. I try not to watch but I can't help being drawn to his face. It's obvious that Wren wants to talk, although he also seems tongue-tied by our shared family history.

"Did you know that there are loads of poisonous plants in the rainforest," he eventually says, letting his left hand trail through a friendly looking clump of ferns. "My favourite is Datura Innoxia, which causes hallucinations and delirium, but you can take your pick. There's a stinging tree with prickly poisonous hairs, and the Wait-a-While has barbed spines, although I think that could be an Australian species, not Amazonian. And that's not to mention all the dangerous creatures like the poison dart frog, rattlesnakes and bullet ants. Or the parasites and bugs in the water. This place is literally crawling with things that just want to eat us or puncture our skin."

"If you're expecting me to protect you, you're out of luck," I say, not sure where this strand of conversation is heading.

Wren almost smiles. "All I'm saying is that there are loads of reasons why we may never make it out of this rainforest. So we might just as well talk to each other, Kaida, because no one else is very interested in either of us."

His use of my name feels way too personal. I glare at him, but his face is calm and serious, he isn't trying to get a rise out of me. It's just my name, after all. I glance at him again. He's now staring straight ahead, leaving it up to me to make the next move.

"Alright," I say, finally giving in. And then I suddenly have no idea what else to say without sounding like a petulant child. I need to change my tone if we're about to have a halfway normal conversation. "So, why did you volunteer anyway?" I ask, just the faintest hint of crabbiness still detectable in my voice.

Wren answers without hesitation. "It was the only way I could earn a place at the Cromwell Institute, my test scores weren't high enough to get me on the captology course," he says with disarming honesty. But it also sounds practised, like he's decided this is the answer he's going to give if anyone asks. It seems we both have secrets to hide. He also seems far too rational and intelligent to risk his life just for a place on a course. He isn't a thrill-seeker either, in fact he's barely shown any enthusiasm for captures, I realise, thinking back to the training room.

"What kind of captures do you want to take, after volunteering?" I ask, genuinely curious about his answer.

"Just normal stuff," Wren says, "archaeology sites, ancient Mayan temples, castle ruins, that sort of thing. What about you?"

I shrug. "I prefer big open landscapes."

Wren nods. We carefully avoid any mention of my sister and his brother. It still feels too raw to bring them into any conversation. I'm not sure we ever will, or if I've got the guts to continue with this newly formed connection. But I'm also surprised at how good it feels to talk to someone. I've already become more lonely and isolated than I've allowed myself to acknowledge.

Wren rejoins the others after another short pause, maybe sensing that it wouldn't be wise to push me too far.

Four hours later, we finally reach our destination and Troy sets everyone to work setting up camp for the night, in a clearing not far from the river. Tents are pegged out, leaves and fronds are cleared to keep small animals and bugs away, and water pouches are hung from the tallest trees. Troy puts me and Pink Hair in charge of building and lighting a large fire, I get it going quickly with the flint and steel from my backpack. Stones are heated in the glowing embers and then used to boil pans of water to rehydrate our food. Night falls so rapidly it's like someone has dimmed the lights on a movie set. Beyond our campsite the darkness is so absolute that anything could be hiding in the trees, or crawling through the undergrowth, just waiting for us to fall asleep and drop our guard. I've seen several documentaries about the rainforest, so I've got some idea about the jaguars that might be stalking us, and the snakes that could slither, unnoticed, into tents and sleeping bags, not to mention a billion mosquitoes and flying bugs that could eat us down to the bone by morning. Just the thought of it makes the skin on my legs and arms itch unbearably.

We sit on our backpacks in a wide circle around the fire for dinner, with the crackling flames and the scraping of metal spoons filling any gaps in our bad tempered conversations. No one likes feeling this exposed and vulnerable.

After dinner, Troy delivers our orders for the next day.

"We'll be hiking through a densely wooded area tomorrow marked on your maps," he says, handing out new worksheets. "This capture is scheduled to be active for a month." Some of the important captures taken for scientific discovery or observation are set out in this way. Stitched together from dozens of different captures, and covering vast areas, they allow for a lengthy time to survey and investigate. "We are just one of half a dozen teams already exploring the forest," he explains, as I flip through the pages, seeing pictures of Spanish Cedars and Mahogany trees two hundred feet tall, with slender leaves and woody seed pods. "You will identify as many of these hardwoods as possible in your allotted areas, and mark their position with your GPS devices."

Nobody else seems surprised by this news, but I am baffled again. Rainforests, like volcanoes, have been explored and studied so extensively that most species of plants and animals have now been identified, their every secret revealed. So why are we looking for hardwood trees, I wonder, when we already know every detail about them?

"Yellabell!" Troy's harsh voice shakes me out of my thoughts and draws a titter of amusement from the other volunteers. "I'm putting you in charge of critter patrol, if anyone finds any poisonous snakes or frogs in the campsite, you will deal with them."

It's obvious that Troy's still punishing me for what happened in the volcano. I can feel his hatred burning through the heat of the campfire between us. I quickly try and calculate the chances of getting through the rest of the capture without being stung or bitten into oblivion. But whichever way I look at it, the odds aren't favourable. How am I supposed to deal with snakes when I can't even remove a spider from the bath at home without backup?

Troy sets up a rota for the night watch, as someone needs to keep an eye on the camp and our equipment at all times. Then I crawl into the tent I'm sharing with Pink Hair. She doesn't even acknowledge my presence, like I'm way beneath her notice, so I hang my mosquito net from a pole, lay my head on my backpack and turn towards the canvas wall for some privacy. I take Grandma Hummingtree's compass from my pocket and hold onto it tightly, trying to think of friendly Northumberland stars. But the uneasy peace doesn't last for long.

9
The Leap

I wake suddenly, aware that there's been a change. Pink Hair is still sleeping, but the agitation of instinct is already trying to rouse her, and she's frowning deeply. I stare around the tent; there's no sign of any rattlesnakes, poison dart frogs or bullet ants attempting to sneak inside. I fumble around for my shoes surprised at how well I can see. It's lighter than when I went to sleep in fact, even though it's the middle of the night, 1.21 a.m. according to my watch.

I crawl out of the tent and it's immediately obvious where the light is coming from. Raven, left in charge of the fire on the first watch of the night, has fallen asleep. He's curled up at a safe distance from the embers, but the fire has spilled out sideways and started to climb the slender trunk of a tree. Long vines, acting like a wick, are drawing flames straight up into the canopy, where there's fresh fuel for the fire to burn, and the whole clearing is now in danger of going up in one big blaze.

I stamp down hard on several glowing embers that float down from above, threatening to set the nearest tents alight, and then I race over to Raven.

"The fire's got out of control, wake up!" I say, my voice sounding monstrously loud.

"What are you doing?" He sits up reluctantly, glaring at me until one thought slowly catches up with another, and he sees the flames crawling up a second and third tree.

"We've got to get everyone up!" I say, but Raven pulls me back.

"Troy will kill me! Help me put the fires out first, Yellabell!" He grabs one of the water pouches and attempts to douse the flames at the base of the third tree. But it's already far too late for fire fighting. The canopy is now fully ablaze, lighting up the night sky like a beacon. Several of the tents have started to smoulder. But the campsite is also quickly coming to life, woken by the urgent tone of our conversation, bodies are already appearing. Troy crawls out into the clearing before I can raise the alarm. Pink Hair emerges looking confused; Rat Face and Blond Spikes huddle together, cowering away from the heat. None of us is exactly good in a crisis.

"Head towards the water!" Troy orders, ignoring Raven's feeble attempts to explain and apologise. "If this fire spreads it will move faster than we can. Leave your backpacks behind!"

More volunteers emerge and Troy hastily rounds everyone up, shoving us all away from the fire and down towards the river. We lurch through the darkness, tripping through the ferns. The fire leaps from treetop to treetop, playing a lethal game of catch. We crash through the forest, stumbling over fallen trees and moss covered rocks, grabbing at vines and palms to steady ourselves on the slippery ground.

I can still hear Troy hollering behind us, instructing everyone to get into the river, away from the fire, which has leapt ahead now, threatening to cut us off before we can reach the cool safety of the water.

I dodge to the left as several blazing palm fronds drop from above, like the sky itself is literally flaking away and burning, like old paint scorched from a door. Sparks scatter in all directions, new fires burst into life, instantly adding to the inferno. Pink Hair and the rest of the volunteers zigzag away from me to the right, but it's too late to change my own course and bridge the gap, fire already divides us. I run hard trying to ignore the sudden terror that being alone brings, hoping I can find everyone else when I reach the river. But the fire has skipped ahead of me, and as I blunder through a dense tangle of knotted vines I'm suddenly confronted by a burning wall of vegetation. I try to double back, picking a new route, and the way is instantly blocked again. More palm fronds drag fire down from the sky, cutting me off, trapping me inside a cage of flames. The skin on my face starts to prickle, sparks smoulder through my clothes and burn out against my skin. Flames circle and prowl around me, waiting for the perfect moment to strike. I need to move quickly but my feet have taken root with the trees and all I can do is watch the forest burn, snake-charmed by the blaze.

"Kaida!" The closeness of the familiar voice startles me. Wren grabs my arm and tugs me urgently towards the only small gap in the cage where escape is still possible. He leaps over a fallen tree just as it catches alight. I follow without hesitation, jumping over the new flames that lick hungrily at my heels. And then we're crashing through the forest before I can even register how close I just came to becoming part of the inferno.

When we finally reach the edge of the river and turn to face the forest, it's obvious there will be no way back. Flames dance up into the night, high above the treetops, like a whole woodland city is burning. It's fierce enough to create a false-dawn sky, bloodshot reds and angry oranges mimicking the rising of the sun.

Wren draws me backwards until we're standing knee deep in water, but the overhanging trees and branches are now in danger of catching alight, forcing us further and further into the black, flowing river.

"We should wade our way round and find the others!" I say, turning into the current, heading upstream. Fire reflects off the surface of the water revealing just how vast and fast-flowing it is. And I have to remind myself that rivers cannot burn, that we are safe and cool and protected. I take it slowly, one uncertain step at a time, avoiding the burning plants which cling to the water's edge and I can feel the current trying to pull me under. There's no sign of the others as we round a bend in the river a few minutes later.

"They must have gone further up, away from the flames," Wren says, undaunted, getting ready to move off again.

But the fire has spread to a small island in a channel of the river, creeping across a thick woody vine. As we move towards it, the vine burns through and drops directly into our path with a burst of glowing sparks. I tilt to my left, trying to avoid the embers, coming down hard on uneven rocks. The river sweeps my feet out from underneath me, like it's been waiting for this moment since we first waded into its depths, and there's nothing I can do to stop it.

"Kaida!" Wren throws himself towards me, trying to grab my arm. But I'm already being hurried downstream and we both get drawn out into a deep water channel, out of the frying pan and into an endless tunnel of darkness.

It's impossible to talk. I dip beneath the surface again and again. My lungs quickly feel choked and frighteningly full, water replacing oxygen whenever I gasp for air. And the heaviness weighs my body down, like my pockets are stuffed full of rocks. I see the dark shape of a boulder rising out of the water, just seconds before the current smashes my body against it. The blow knocks the last reserves of air out of my lungs and I know how this is going to end, unless my lucky stars are watching over us both. I catch confusing glimpses of Wren away to my left side, arms flailing, chin tilted upwards, but it's almost completely dark now and the river is showing no signs of letting us drift into the shallows. My leg catches on another hidden jag of rock, this time the skin tears beneath my clothes with a sharp sting. Wren spins away from me to the left, propelled into a different channel of the river, and then for the second time in one terrifying night, I'm completely alone.

Fear and panic make me gasp and flail with ever greater desperation, until I finally sink beneath the surface, descending into the black depths, too exhausted to keep up the fight. My lungs instantly begin to protest at the lack of oxygen and it feels like I'm slowly suffocating. Long chains of bubbles escape from my mouth and nose, rising back up to the surface and salvation. I watch the bubbles helplessly, letting the water carry me on its own path, rag-doll limp, drifting without resistance.

For one brief moment it's almost peaceful. I can sense the comforting presence of Millie in the darkness beside me and I know she won't leave me to face this alone, that she'll stay with me to the very end and beyond. I feel the touch of her warm hand as she grasps my fingers and holds on tight. I let my eyes close, just for a second, so I can concentrate on our last moments together...

The current spins me abruptly, shunting me into another channel. My feet hit the riverbed, forcing me to stagger and lurch until I'm knee deep, and I can stand on both feet without the danger of being dragged under again. Water gushes out of my nose. I choke on the regurgitation of river and then manage to force some air into my starved lungs. Every breath stabs at my chest like I've snapped several ribs or inhaled some prickly thorns. I'm learning how to breathe all over again, but the rhythmic heaving of my chest soon starts to soothe and calm, and I finally believe that I'm not going to drown.

I see a small light bobbing along the water's edge towards me. Wren! Two time survivor. Two days he'll never forget if he defies our current odds and lives long enough for memories. The torchlight catches the reflective strips on my arms and legs and he's suddenly crashing through the water. I'm so relieved to see him, so relieved that we've both survived the river, that we're both still breathing air. He drags me back to the riverbank where I sit and cough, heaving up every last drop of water, and it burns the lining of my throat and nose. I hug my sides, unable to prevent the great sobs that now shake every part of my already buffeted body. And I let the tears come. Better to get it out now than to bottle it away, where it can ferment and corrode inside.

"I thought you'd been swept away," Wren says, his voice sounding choked and unsteady, and it's obvious that he's been crying too.

I nod, some of the sobs returning briefly, but I've almost got it under control now, and I take a few slow breaths while he checks me over with his torch for damage.

"You've got a nasty cut on your leg," he says, sitting me upright and leaning me against the slope of the bank. He tears the material away and inspects the injury more closely. It's a deep gouge, three inches long and bleeding heavily. If the river is filled with bacteria, there's a good chance it could become infected, and all our medical supplies have been left at the campsite. We're not out of danger yet.

We have to get back to the others. We're not the only team in the rainforest; they won't pull the capture just because two volunteers have gone missing. That's supposedly what we signed up for. If we can't find Troy before he leads everyone else out of here, we'll have to survive on our own for a whole month, until the scheduled end date of the capture. I try not to think about how impossible a mission that would be. Just finding enough clean water to drink would be a daily do or die task.

"Stay here," Wren says. "I'll be back in a minute."

I'm left in total darkness again. Now that I've escaped from the river, the solitude is truly frightening, so I stare up at the stars and try to focus on the friendly points of light they offer. I can no longer hear the roaring of the campsite fire, no trace of burning flames lights up the sky, so we must have been carried some distance down the river. I check my watch, 2.42 a.m. Another few hours until the sun comes up and we can see how far we've drifted away from the rest of the group.

Wren returns, splashing through the shallows, carrying a fistful of leaves. He hands me the torch as he crushes the leaves, which release a sticky salve that looks like slug slime. "Indigenous people have been using these leaves for hundreds of years to treat cuts, and stop them getting infected," he says.

"How come you know so much about plants in the rainforest?" I ask, watching him take the torn strip of material from my suit, using it to bind the leaves to my leg. It feels deliciously cool and soothing, if nothing else it will help stop the bleeding. The last thing I need is to leave a bloody trail for every flesh-hungry creature in the rainforest to salivate over.

"I like reading about plants," Wren says. "It's sort of a hobby, but I want to study botany at university when I'm old enough."

"I thought you wanted to be a captologist? Isn't that why you volunteered?"

"Right, a botanical captologist," Wren says, trying to make it sound like an actual thing. But it's obvious that captology isn't his first choice. I consider asking if he too was the victim of a faked capture, if he's here against his will, but I hold my tongue, conscious that we could be under observation right now, and since I still don't know who I can trust...

"Thanks for saving me from the fire," I say, my voice wobbling dangerously again.

"I think that means we're even now," Wren says, with no hint of a smile. "I also think we should both stay away from any naked flames in the future, neither of us is exactly fire-proof."

We find a clearing just beyond the banks of the river where I ignore Wren's wise words, and quickly start a small blaze. There's plenty of tinder to burn, and I've still got the flint and steel in my pocket from lighting the campfire earlier. The flames make our surroundings marginally less terrifying and help to give us a much needed source of light, before the batteries in Wren's torch fail. We remove our sodden shoes and socks, hanging them on sticks over the flames, hoping they might dry out a little, and then we do an inventory of our resources. It doesn't amount to much. No food, no drinking water, no emergency flares, not that Troy would waste time coming to rescue us anyway, he's already made his feelings on the subject clear. What we do have is Grandma Hummingtree's compass and a small map. We spend some time studying the map by torchlight, trying to work out how far down the river we might have come, but it's difficult to tell for sure in the darkness. It's also impossible to concentrate on anything with hundreds of midges and biting insects swarming around us, feasting on every millimetre of bare skin. Wren scoops out handfuls of mud from the river shallows and we paint ourselves from head to toe with the cool slippery substance, working it into our hair, over noses, ears, lips and eyelids, until no speck of skin is left exposed and vulnerable. And then an awkward silence falls between us.

Except for the last few hours, when communication has been a necessary survival tool, we've barely spoken to each other. Now there's no way to avoid the inevitable conversation that's hanging over us, with the darkness, like a hood. But with our faces camouflaged and hidden by mud, it's also the perfect time to broach the impossible subject.

"Do you—" I start then stop, not sure how to phrase the question.

"Do I what?" Wren raises a muddy eyebrow at me, which causes the protective layer to crack. He reapplies a fresh glob smoothing it into his skin.

"Do you remember much about your brother?" I ask, staring at my feet, hugging my wet knees closely to my chest, being careful not to touch the leafy dressing on my leg.

Wren takes a long slow breath and then huffs it out, like he doesn't know how to have this conversation either. "I remember playing dinosaurs with him in my bedroom. I was obsessed with the whole Jurassic era when I was younger. And Kit did a really good Tyrannosaurus Rex." Wren adds his own muted impression. "*Grrrrr.*" His fingers curling round like pretend animal claws.

It's impossible not to smile. And in the tiny, private, fire-tinted world we've created, it's also easy to imagine a much younger Wren, laughing gleefully, as his brother stomps around pretending to be a big, bad, hungry carnivore.

"Me and Kit had this whole made-up dinosaur world called Rexodinium." Wren stares into the flames, thumbing his eyebrow absently as he talks. "Kit was always the T-Rex because he was the oldest and the tallest. And I was always the very unlucky caveman who got chased, or mauled to death, or chased and *then* mauled to death, and I loved every minute of it."

His voice is filled with sadness and affection, the loss of his brother still playing a major part in his life. And I know exactly what he's been through, the intense emotions he's experiencing now, as he pictures a brother who will never be a part of any family outing, gathering or argument again. Wren's loss is just as acute as mine, and I'm suddenly ashamed that I've never realised it before. I am the one person in the world who he does not have to explain his feelings to. I don't need to ask if he still dreams about Kit, or feels the presence of his brother treading softly through the fading shadows of sleep. I already know that Wren does a regular inventory of all the precious memories he holds, so that none are ever forgotten, each detail preserved forever, recalled without effort or distortion. It now seems ridiculous that we've never spoken to each other before about the loss we've both shared. But can we ever get beyond the traumatic circumstances that took both Kit and Millie away?

I draw circles in the mud on my legs where it's still moist and river warm, another disturbing thought emerging with uncomfortable clarity. I have always hated being compared to Millie, as if I somehow couldn't exist without her presence blazing a trail before me. And yet I've done exactly the same thing to Wren, smeared him with the shame of his brother's crimes, without ever giving him a chance to prove his own worth, which he's already done. Without him, I would be dead, consumed by flames.

I shiver and snatch a quick look at Wren. He's lost in his own thoughts, his sad expression visible even through the mask of mud he wears. And I realise that as hard as I've tried to keep him at arm's length, he's somehow made a favourable impression on me anyway. He's kind, brave and intelligent, none of the things I was expecting him to be. I wonder if his opinion of me falls on the favourable side. Apart from inside the volcano, have I done anything to make him think well of me?

The night drags on. We pass the time until dawn by talking about the other volunteers, which ones we find most irritating, which ones we'd most like to cast adrift in a swamp full of alligators. Neither of us is brave enough to ask more about Kit and Millie and then the rain falls, hard and loud, removing any need for conversation, but it provides no relief from the heat. I try to catch some of the drops in my mouth, head tilted backwards. It tastes as sweet as the rotting fruit on the forest floor, but at least it eases the burning in my throat.

When the sky shifts from black to grey, and then to a startling, mottled pink, we can finally study the map and use my compass to identify the distinctive dogleg bend in the river where we're sitting. It's a good few miles back to the camp. If we're lucky, we might find Troy and the rest of our group still picking through the burnt remains of the fire, before they set off on their assignment.

I take the lead first, setting a swift pace, despite the weeping cut on my leg, which burns with every step. We travel along the edge of the river, using the compass to keep on course and I wonder if my lucky talisman helped keep us both alive again. The terrain is hard going, clogged with twisted roots and unstable river stones, just made for trips and stumbles. We're both ravenously hungry now that most of the shock has worn off, but neither of us knows enough about the plants in the forest to risk gathering roots or berries. After two hours, I finally catch sight of the blackened trees, a scar in the landscape where the fire took hold, where all colour and life has been extinguished.

We head inland again, picking our way slowly over the charred ground, still hot underfoot despite the recent rain, and our shoes stick to the black-tar residue. When we reach the campsite it's deserted, tent frames have been bent like broken stems, rucksacks burnt to piles of blackened ash. It's obvious that the site has been picked clean of anything worth salvaging and then abandoned. A trail heads south through the forest, trampled by many feet.

"The sun's only been up for a couple of hours," I say, staring up through a big hole in the canopy, destroyed by the fire. "Maybe we can still catch up."

"If that's the right trail to follow, it could have been made by another group at another time."

But we decide it's worth the risk. It's the only real chance we've got. Wren takes the lead this time, drawn by the promise of food and fresh water, but it's getting harder to keep up the pace on an empty stomach and a body deprived of sleep. My legs feel heavier and heavier as we tramp in silence, my cut now bleeding freely. And we both need to take ever more frequent breaks before moving off again. The path begins to narrow the further we trek into the forest, until the way ahead has been all but reclaimed by the trees.

"Stop!" Wren suddenly grabs my wrist, his arm shooting out sideways to form a barrier.

He doesn't need to explain the note of alarm in his voice. We've reached a cliff edge, hidden by a line of trees that cling to the lip of a rocky outcrop. One step further and we would have plummeted over the edge into the green canopy now spread out beneath us. The trees are so tall I could almost reach out and pluck a handful of leaves.

"We must have followed the wrong trail," I say, taking several steps backwards, surveying the landscape. The whole forest is now laid out before us and I can see for miles in every direction. After being trapped under the oppressive canopy for so long, it's a relief to be out in the open again, to catch more than just a few glimpses of the sky, like a lid has been lifted. I stare into the distance, focusing on the point where the trees meet the clear blue sky, before I survey the forest closest to us. The river is now several hundred metres away. There's no sign of any ropes or ladders that could have been used to climb down from our elevated dead end. But in the distance, at the water's edge under the trees...

"Hey, that's Pink Hair!" I say pointing to the head I can clearly see, a stark contrast against the green of the forest. The whole group, in fact, is lined up along the river bank next to two boats that they're filling with backpacks and supplies, obviously rescued from the campsite.

"They're leaving," Wren says and we both understand what this means. By the time we've found a safe route down from the cliff, back through the forest to the river, they will be long gone, oblivious to our desperate attempts to reach them.

Wren sucks in a huge lungful of air and lets out an ear-splitting yell, hands cupped around his mouth for extra volume. We both shout, trying to attract attention, leaping and waving our arms with the last of our energy, but no one can hear us over the noise of the river that they're standing so close to.

"We've got to climb down," I say, realising it's the only way to reach our group in time.

Wren peers carefully over the edge of the cliff, studying the trees beneath us. It's a huge risk, one bad landing could mean broken arms, legs or wrists, and then our chances of survival would nosedive. There's no guarantee that the spindly branches in the treetops can even support our weight. I wonder for a moment if my judgement is being impaired by lack of sleep, water and food, and if jumping into the canopy is the craziest decision ever. But even if it is, we have to try.

"There!" Wren points to one of the tallest trees with an umbrella-shaped crown. "That's a Kapok tree, it's strong and it's covered in thorns, we might be able to use them to climb down the trunk. Wrap your hands in something to shield the skin."

I take off my shoes and use my damp, grungy socks, bandaging my hands for protection, trying not to think about the thorns. Then there's nothing left to do but leap, there's no time to work up any courage either, this is a one jump deal and my worst nightmare. It makes the hole in the metal walkway look like a cakewalk.

"Together?" Wren suggests, grabbing my sock-covered hand. It doesn't even feel strange after the closeness we've forged from our night of near-death experience, fire and mud. And I grip his fingers in return with feverish resolve.

"On the count of three," I say, shifting my weight between my feet, trying to un-stick them from the ground. "One, two, *three!*"

Wren leaps high, launching himself into nothingness, his limbs spread out wide like a flying squirrel, using his easy graceful movements to help him. My trajectory is lower and blunter, my hand instantly wrenched out of Wren's as I belly flop into the canopy. I crash through the thin upper branches, which strike my face and snap against my body. But I'm too amped-up on adrenaline to notice any pain. Seed pods rupture all around me and I'm quickly covered in Kapok fluff, my face feels like a burst cushion and I can't breathe without choking. But nothing slows me down, and I continue to tumble at an alarming rate through a fog of green leaves and branches. I drop straight through the bottom edge of the canopy, where I smash against the thick trunk. Thorns slice through my clothes like razors, but I finally come to a halt, a bluebottle caught in fly paper.

"Kaida! Are you okay?" Flying Squirrel Boy calls urgently from somewhere above me.

"Just a few broken bones!" I say, spitting fluff, and I'm only half joking, because it feels like I've been battered by an army of broom handles.

I cling to the tree with my feet, squeezing the trunk between my knees, hands groping for a more secure hold and then I stare over my shoulder. It's still a terrifying drop to the ground. A rush of fear travels all the way down to the soles of my feet and I tighten my grip on the tree, feeling sick with dizziness, but there's no turning back now. I can't exactly climb up to the ridge and try again.

I wait until Wren has clambered down to my level, trying to stop my arms and legs from shaking. Then we descend the rest of the way together. The thorns are brutal and mortally sharp, if I lose my grasp now, I'll be grated to shreds before I can slither to the bottom. But they also offer foot and handholds when approached with caution, and I use them as best I can, keeping three points of contact with the tree at all times. The tough material of my clothes provides some protection, but not even that can save me from the scrapes and cuts that I collect like climbing trophies. Wren flinches away from the thorns and we both leave a trail of fresh blood and angry curses behind us.

When we're finally reunited with solid ground, all I want to do is hug the tree roots and the rocks and listen to the steady, comforting hum of the world as it turns. But we have to push on before the rest of our group sails down the river without us. We're close enough now to hear the echo of familiar voices and we crash through the forest making as much noise as possible. I spot a flash of pink hair through the trees ahead, and I've never been so pleased to see such a sour-faced girl in my life.

Even Pink Hair can't hide her utter shock as we burst through the edge of the forest, and stand panting and sweating and bleeding before her.

"We thought you two were dead," she says folding her arms, frowning at the white fluff that covers our clothes and clings to our hair, making us both look like leftovers from a Halloween parade.

I grab two water bottles from a pile on a rock and throw one to Wren. I down the liquid without pausing for breath and then take another. It tastes like the contents of a warm bath that's had the pleasure of cleaning a series of muddy dogs, but I drink until my throat is no longer as dry as a roll of ancient parchment. Pink Hair tells us the assignment has been abandoned, because most of the equipment and supplies were damaged or destroyed in the fire, and that they're taking a shorter route back to the capture entry point along the river.

When word reaches Troy that we've made it back from the brink, he storms over with a face like a thundercloud and demands to know where we've been; like we deliberately let the river take us miles downstream for our own amusement. Wren explains quickly, sticking to the facts as Braided Hair, Rat Face, Blond Spikes and the others crowd round to listen, no one asks if we're injured or in any need of help or food. Their lack of basic human concern is kind of upsetting, even though it doesn't surprise me. Team spirit has never flowed between us with abundance.

Troy doesn't even attempt to hide his disappointment that we're still alive. But short of marching us back into the forest, tying us to a tree and letting jaguars feast on our internal organs, there's nothing he can do about it. We board the boat fifteen minutes later and not even the droning noise of the motor can stop me from falling into an exhausted stupor. But two stubborn thoughts refuse to fade into oblivion. Why is Troy so angry that we're still alive? And what is he planning to do about it?

10
Delivery

An hour later, we eventually reach the changing room outside the capture booth, and Troy announces that we now have three days off before our next assignment. I haven't got enough energy left to take part in the backslapping, hugging and celebrations that follow. Me and Wren join the tail end of a queue instead, behind Rat Face and Raven, and wait our turn to be seen by a doctor before we leave the sublevels. Doctor Varner listens to the water crackles in my lungs, then she inspects the cut on my leg, giving me an injection of strong antibiotics. She supplies me with a tub of cream for the impressive collection of scrapes and gouges that cover the rest of my body. And three bars of high calorie energy cake, which she instructs me to eat while she's cleaning and dressing my wound properly. She doesn't waste any time on sympathy or reassurance. I wait until Wren has been given his own creams and ointments, and we make our way back up to the living quarters together, in virtual silence, a ragtag sight in our charred clothes, overlaid with a swamp-monster finish.

"Can I call round sometime tomorrow?" Wren asks nervously as my hand rests on the door to my room. "There's something I really need to talk to you about."

"Okay," I say, wondering if he wants to take the plunge and discuss Kit and Millie. If he does, I've decided not to shy away from it. After everything we've been through together, I owe him at least one conversation on the sensitive subject, no matter how awkward and upsetting.

I smile briefly at Wren before disappearing into my room, not sure what footing we're now on; friends, fellow survivors, no longer linked by our shared history alone?

I slump onto my bed feeling like I need two weeks, minimum, to recover from our ordeal in the rainforest. The scratches on my arms and legs cover a network of insect bites that itch insanely. I've got more bruises than a bucket full of windfall apples. My volunteer clothes are caked in dried sweat, river mud and other unsavoury residues. I drag myself to my feet again and hit the shower with my clothes still on, it's quicker than going to the laundry, I'm not sure they'd survive the spin cycle anyway, and I'm too exhausted to find out. Cool water helps ease the itching, I have to shampoo my hair three times to remove all the sun-baked mud and river silt, but I finally crawl into my wonderfully clean, bug-free bed. It's only 7.03 p.m., according to my alarm clock. I haven't been to bed this early since I was eight years old, but my body doesn't care, it needs rest, and it needs it now. I fall asleep in the time it takes to pull the duvet over my head, all troubling thoughts and fears numbed by overwhelming fatigue.

Hunger wakes me early the next morning and the gnawing emptiness in my stomach is too persistent to ignore. But I'm not going to waste a single second of my precious three days off. I message Hekla then have another long shower and head gingerly up to the almost deserted cafeteria. Every muscle and bone in my body protests at the slightest movement, even my toes are sore from my tree-hugging descent, and I have to hobble like an old woman, or pay the consequences. I pile my plate high at the food counter with double eggs, bacon, sausage, buttered toast and a huge blueberry muffin that looks too lonely to leave behind. It only makes up for a few of the meals I've missed but it's a good place to start, and I take my time, savouring the flavours.

As soon as I've finished, I gently climb the stairs in the far corner that lead out onto the rooftop garden. A strong blast of damp air hits me as soon as I open the door, but I'll take a grey December day in London over a tropical nightmare, any time of the year. I stand with my coat flapping open just letting the breeze reach all the parts of me that still feel overheated. Then I shuffle past the dog walkers, all bundled up in their heavy coats and hats, ignoring the queue at the gondola, and cut through the arboretum to the Japanese Tea Garden, where I've arranged to meet Hekla. At this time of year, it's usually deserted, due to the open-air nature of the cafe. But I've always liked the red painted pagoda and the high arch of the single bridge that spans the frozen lily pond. Hekla is already waiting, her arms folded tightly across the puffed jacket she's wearing, her shoulders hunched up around her ears against the winter chill.

"This is the dumbest idea you've ever had! What's wrong with Nyman's or the Copper-Bottomed Cafe, they've both got four walls and a roof, and central heating," she says, as I take a seat beside her, lowering myself into the chair delicately. She's already ordered a pot of tea which is sitting untouched in front of her. "And there's something seriously wrong with this tea," she complains, removing the lid and glaring at the contents, which she prods suspiciously with a spoon. "Shouldn't it be black, not all green and gunky? It looks like someone's stewed a heap of snot."

I can't help smiling as Hekla shivers and fidgets; it's a relief to have such a normal conversation after the intensity of the last few days, and I relish her teapot dramas. I'm so pleased to see her I just sit silently as she orders a hot chocolate and a huge slice of chocolate cherry cake instead, with two forks.

"So, how's the volunteering?" she eventually asks, studying me carefully, struggling to keep the worried big-sister scowl off her face. And I pull my coat sleeves down over the cuts and insect bites on my hands. "You look like you've caught the sun or something."

"Yeah, they've been sending us to all the most glamorous tropical island resorts, so we can lounge around on the beach and drink water from coconuts."

Hekla rolls her eyes, but she's not laughing. "Seriously, where have you been, because you're sort of singed?" She traces the line of my left eyebrow gently with her finger to demonstrate. It's half an inch shorter than it used to be, with nothing but a fuzz of black stubble at one end.

I fill her in quickly on the volcano and the rainforest, not lingering on any of the details, because if Hekla is too appalled or worried for my life, it will somehow make the whole experience much harder to endure. So I skip the parts about rescuing Wren and being swept down a parasite infested river. I can tell she's onto me though. She knows that I'm not telling her everything, but she doesn't try and force the issue, and I'm grateful that I don't have to relive every near-death experience I've had in the last few days.

"Have you been staying away from the weedy McKenzie kid, like I told you to?" she asks when I've finally finished.

"I haven't even spoken to him, everyone hates him." It's an uncomfortable lie, I can usually tell Hekla anything and I hate the way this conversation is making me feel. But I'm not sure she'll understand the strange situation me and Wren now find ourselves in, unless I fill her in on everything else.

"Well, I've been doing some research into Tobias Troy," she says, shovelling three huge forkfuls of cake into her mouth before chewing. She pulls up a newsfeed on her phone and shows me a report of Scrim and Cassian Cromwell meeting the new volunteers. "It was so weird seeing you on TV, I almost choked on my breakfast eggs when I saw it."

"You've been eating plain old eggs for breakfast?" I joke, trying to sound equally shocked at her unusually healthy choice of food.

Hekla grins. "Joke all you want, I'm not the one who's properly famous now. The whole thing about you and Wren being volunteers together has gone super viral. I watched a sixty minute debate last night about whether you two are mortal enemies now, just like Kit and Millie."

I'm suddenly glad I've been hidden away from all the intrusive interest and speculation. I watch the news report, cringing at the sight of myself and how young and frightened I look standing next to Rilla, Pink Hair and everyone else.

"It's so obvious that Scrim doesn't want Cassian anywhere near you," Hekla says, replaying the moment several times over where Scrim steers him away from my end of the line. "She could probably see that crazy look on your face. But that's not the most interesting part; just take a look at Troy." Hekla has to point him out as he's almost hidden in the shadows in the far corner of the shot, keeping his distance, standing close to the supply cupboards.

"He must have crept in to watch us before Roth introduced him as our team leader," I say, puzzling over his presence.

Instead of focusing on Scrim and Cassian Cromwell like everyone else, Troy's eyes never leave me. He studies me with the look of someone contemplating how to slaughter a troublesome pig. It's highly unnerving, but it adds some weight to my growing suspicion that he'd be more than happy if I was the next casualty in our volunteer group.

"Anyway, I did some rootling around and I've found out a few choice details about him," Hekla says, squirming in her chair, itching to tell me what she's discovered. "He lives alone for a start."

"I'm not surprised. Even a vial full of Martian bacteria would think twice before setting up home with that moron."

Hekla stares at me, blinking. "Don't hold back, say what you really think."

89

"If you met him you'd understand," I say, knowing she'd despise him as much as I do.

"Well he's got no family," Hekla continues, "he's never been married, no kids or pets. And judging by some very ugly end of term school reports, written years ago by one of his old housemasters, I wouldn't be totally shocked if he ate puppies and kittens for breakfast."

I smile at the instant Cruella De Vil image that pops into my head.

"He trained here at the Institute, volunteered when he was eighteen and he's been head volunteer team leader for twelve years now. His face was all over the media when that ancient capture machine was stolen from the Institute. Scrim put him in charge of the internal investigation, no trace of it was ever found. But he did catch someone down in the sublevels once, who was making dark captures."

Everyone's heard the stories about dark captures. Unofficial and anonymous, they're taken by rogue captologists who steal from the Cromwells, and then sell their skills to the highest bidder. Dark captures allegedly expose top governmental secrets, or unravel age-old mysteries, or catch powerful people doing unsavoury things they've always denied. Their existence is almost mythical, like the lost city of Atlantis or Robin Hood. They surface only on rare occasions and are swiftly removed from the public domain by the Cromwells. Not even Hekla has ever seen a dark capture, although she'd love to get her hands on one of the juicier examples that claims to expose the existence of aliens, or provides proof that the original Cassian Cromwell is still alive and kicking, over a hundred years after he supposedly died.

"The most interesting thing I've found out about Troy is that during his time as a team leader, the number of volunteers has doubled," Hekla tells me.

"Doubled?" It's certainly not due to his magnetic personality or sparkling people skills. "So you think Troy is using fake captures to force people into volunteering, and that's why the numbers are up?"

Hekla shrugs. "It's just a theory. But if Troy is involved, he must be paying a brilliant techie to fake captures for him, there's no way he could even attempt to do it on his own. I've seen his IQ test scores and he's not exactly an evil genius."

We both sit silently thinking over the idea as Hekla finishes her cake, scooping the last morsels off the plate with her fingers.

"If Troy is faking captures, how do we prove it?" I ask.

"I've been trying to hack into his personal accounts. I figured he might be dumb enough to brag about faking captures to one of his mates, or message someone in the tech labs," Hekla explains, licking her fingers, one by one. "But he's using a special encryption and it's taking me ages to crack the code. In the meantime, stay as far away from him as possible," she warns, all joking and teasing suddenly gone. "Because Troy's the closest thing I've found to a psychopath."

We only leave the cafe when the cold finally gets too much for both of us. It's hard saying goodbye, especially as I have a horrible dread that the next capture assignment will prove deadly, and this will be the last time I ever see my best and oldest friend. I hug her tightly only letting go when she complains that I'm squashing her eyeballs. Hekla goes home to do more digging into Troy, with a promise to update me with any new discoveries via LondonCall.

I'm planning to spend the next few hours slathering my cuts and bruises with cool cream, and then catching up on some sleep. But when I unlock my door back in the living quarters, I see an open box sitting on my bed, a box that definitely wasn't there when I left. Someone has been in my room.

I quickly check the door for signs of a break-in, and cast a wary eye over my belongings, but nothing has been disturbed. My clothes are still heaped on the floor like grubby termite mounds; everything is exactly as I left it — apart from the mysterious box.

I prop the door open with my bag and approach the box cautiously, in case it's some kind of cruel joke sent by the other volunteers, booby-trapped with cockroaches or snakes. But I can quickly see that it contains nothing organic, and that the only things sitting inside it are three sleek black canisters. My breath catches in my chest at the sight of the time captures. Cockroaches and snakes would have been less dangerous.

I listen, trying to work out if I've just been set-up again, if I've already triggered some kind of alarm that will end with me being escorted to Scrim's office, for another humiliating trial. But no stray scents of cooking fat reach me, no one appears in the open doorway behind me, so I nudge my bag with my foot, allowing the door to close. There's something else sitting at the bottom of the box, I realise, as I edge closer. A pale cream-coloured envelope addressed to me, *Little Dragon*. The handwriting is bold, a large looping scrawl...and I'd recognise it anywhere.

I snatch up the note, all caution gone, and walk swiftly over to the window where there's more light to read by. The envelope looks crinkled like it's been stuffed inside the box for years. My fingers are now shaking so badly that it takes me several attempts to extract the short note sealed inside.

Dear Kaida,
Watch these captures in this order, 100090, 100145, 100008. You'll need
boots and a warm coat. DO NOT show them to anyone else.
I miss you, Little Dragon. I wish I was there with you.
Millie xxxx

I read the note again, hearing Millie's animated voice inside my head, the first wonderful words I've heard from her in six long years. And then I remember. Today is the sixth anniversary of my sister's death. With everything else that's been going on I'd completely forgotten this most important date. It's only after six years that remaining family members are allowed to see captures of the departed. Some think this rule is cruel and unnecessary, that the mourning family should be allowed to see their loved ones as soon and as often as they want, to help with the grieving process. But the restriction has saved many from wasting away with the dead. Normally, at fifteen years old, I wouldn't be allowed to receive any captures from the archives. And this delivery from Millie would have been sent on my sixteenth birthday. But my status as a volunteer has changed all of that. It's one of the only perks that my new life has brought.

A slip of paper has been tucked in behind her note. It's a copy of a capture request form, filled out by Millie just five weeks before her death, according to the date. It's far more normal for capture requests to be placed electronically, they then go through a central system that automatically grants or rejects the application, based on the age of the person, and the content of the captures being asked for. Paper requests however, are handled by a single person, in the archives, using their own judgement and common sense. Millie wanted to get these captures to me without anyone noticing, I realise, without setting off any alarm bells. She's sending me a message, one that she believed was worth a very long wait. My heart begins to beat painfully hard inside my chest because the appearance of these captures begs the awful question; did Millie know what was coming? Is that why she went to all the trouble of requesting these captures? Is that why I often feel she's trailing somewhere behind me, just out of sight, because she had one last message to give?

I tie my hair back hastily, scraping the scabs off a row of insect bites embedded in my scalp, as I secure the ponytail with two pins. I pull my heaviest snow boots on, ignoring a swoop of nerves in my stomach. Then I scoop up the canisters, grab my coat, with a hat, scarf and gloves already stuffed into the deep pockets, and hurry out of my room again, all thoughts of sleep and my aching body forgotten. I head straight for the Long Walk and then hurry impatiently up the stairs to the flat. The college booths are far too open and public, a paradise for prying eyes, the only way to guarantee any privacy is to see these captures at home.

The flat is empty, Yarena's still at work. Measles greets me warmly as I stop in the kitchen first for a peanut butter sandwich and a tall glass of milk to keep me fuelled, a sensible precaution as I have no idea what I'm about to encounter. The flat feels so reassuring and friendly that some of the tension leaves my body. And while I eat my sandwich, I listen to the soothing tick of the calendar clock and the familiar hum of the fridge, like old friends I've come to visit. Then I make my way through Yarena's office and up to the rooftop booth. It smells like a leafy day in autumnal woods, and it's obvious that Yarena has used it recently. But I barely register the aroma. I load the first capture according to Millie's instructions; the screen above the door takes several seconds to show any details, and then all it gives me is a recommendation for sturdy footwear. It also tells me this capture is set in observation mode.

I pull open the door and wait impatiently for the capture to emerge, hoping that both me and our ancient booth can cope with whatever I'm about to discover. I recognise the bare bedrock walls instantly. I'm somewhere in the sublevels at the Institute, with the familiar smell of nervous volunteers and fresh survival supplies in the air. This first capture was taken in a large training room, empty and innocuous looking apart from a group of volunteers all huddled together at the back, ten feet from where I'm now standing. Several instructors are shouting conflicting orders, including Bulldog Woman who is organising a group of anxious volunteers into a line. This is a training session of some kind, caught on capture, but none of the volunteers are familiar to me. I can't work out what any of this has got to do with my sister, until I notice an opening in the wall at the far side. It leads directly into another training room. Even from this distance I recognise Cyrus Roth, he's clearly delivering a lecture to a different group of volunteers, one of whom has distinctive silvery hair. I feel a nervous thrill at the sudden glimpse of Millie. It's obvious that the conversation she wants me to listen to is happening in that room, caught accidentally in the background, while another capture was being taken.

There's just one problem. At the exact same moment as I take a step towards the other side of the room, the rest of the volunteers begin their training session around me, and I'm suddenly knocked off my feet by something resembling a boxer's punching bag. I land, winded, flat on my back, all my injuries from the rainforest now pulsing with second day pain. I lie motionless for several minutes, not sure if I'm still in the firing line. All I can hear is the heavy thump of other volunteers being struck by more bags that descend from a rig on the ceiling. Attached to long chains, the bags spin wildly, causing total mayhem. Bulldog Woman is yelling instructions about how to avoid being clobbered, but judging by the disgruntled sounds echoing around the room, nobody is making a very good job of it. The capture ends before I can get my breath back or struggle to my feet again. And I know I'll have to reload it if I'm going to find out why Millie wanted me to hear the conversation taking place in the far room.

This time, I stand safely on the sidelines, until all the punching bags have revealed their positions. I watch as they career around like violent spinning tops, changing direction each time they collide with a hapless volunteer, until they've toppled everyone in the room again. And I wonder what this training session is supposed to prepare them for.

When I load the capture for a third time, I'm ready to take my chances again. I manage to dodge my way to the centre of the room before I'm struck from behind, and end up face first, nose pressed hard into the ground. There's no sign of blood, so nothing is broken or badly injured, I'm grateful I've still got all my teeth, but my whole face now aches.

On my next attempt, I have to dive to the floor to avoid being wiped out again, but I make it to the other side with nothing but sore knees. There's no time to catch my breath, I have to pick up everything I'm supposed to hear now, as there's no way I'm braving the punching bags again. I enter the room where Roth is delivering his cheerful welcome speech, and I realise this must be Millie's first day as a volunteer. I move carefully through the group until I'm standing beside her, our shoulders brushing together.

This is the first time I've been in the same room as my sister for six long years. I'd always planned to borrow any capture that she'd been part of, as soon as I was old enough; I'd already tried to imagine how it would feel to see her again. But nothing could have prepared me for this profound sense of relief, the easing of an uncomfortable pressure inside my chest that I hadn't even been aware of until this moment. It's incredible to be in her living presence, even if that presence is nothing more than a ghost. I can't stop the tears that come but I brush them away swiftly with the back of my hand. I don't want to miss anything.

Her hair is shorter than I remember; she's wearing her favourite necklace, a small jet-black pendant shaped like a bumble bee. The expression on her face is more eloquent than any Shakespearean play, she's as angry as thunder, arms folded across her chest, scowl aimed directly at Roth. This is not where she wants to be, and anyone standing within a ten foot radius could pick up the signals she's emitting on a livid, cross-me-if-you-dare frequency. When Roth asks her directly why she volunteered, she glares at everyone in the room before answering.

"Why do you care?"

Every other volunteer stares at her with open admiration and amazement, but I can't help smiling. Millie was never afraid of answering back to anyone. If Cassian Cromwell himself had asked her the same question, he would have got an identical response. She was fearless when it came to sticking up for herself, or anyone else she cared about. But she never did it for effect, only if she had a good reason, so I listen carefully to what comes next.

"You will give me a proper answer, Miss Hummingtree," Roth says, only just managing to keep a lid on his surprise. "I will not tolerate insolence in my training room."

"Alright, the truth is I didn't volunteer, I'd rather work in a toenail gathering facility than be here, in your training room," she says with perfect delivery, in her practised actor's voice.

The large veins in Roth's neck are beginning to throb, and his face is turning a shade of puce that clashes brilliantly with the hint of red in his stubble. But Millie tilts her chin upwards in defiance, unafraid, the battle only just beginning.

"I will ask you one more time, if you'd rather be handling toenails, as you so politely put it, why did you volunteer?"

"I've already told you, I didn't, somebody volunteered me, I didn't have a choice," she says loudly and clearly. But Roth obviously doesn't believe her, taking it as a refusal to answer his question. He's barging through the others to confront her face-to-face, when the capture ends abruptly, the punching bag session coming to a close in the room behind me. This is as much of the conversation as I'm ever going to hear, but it's enough to understand why Millie wanted me to experience this capture. I now know for certain that she didn't volunteer, someone faked a capture that gave her a choice of this, or jail.

I stand in the empty capture booth, taking a moment to relive everything that's just happened, the warm feeling of being in my sister's presence once again, the sheer, indescribable delight of standing beside her, of hearing her voice. And then I exit the booth and load the next capture, taken three months after the first one, according to the date on the canister.

The air around me shifts and alters as I step back inside, closing the door, and I'm plunged into sudden darkness. It's also iceberg cold so I pull on my hat and coat, yanking the hood over my head to protect my ears from the instant wind-chill, wrapping my scarf around my neck. This time, I'm standing outside, on the slope of a hill, almost knee-deep in pristine snow. Fat heavy flakes fall like ghosts from the sky and I'm surrounded by tall fir trees, bowed by the weight of their snowy caps, until they resemble sinister hooded figures. There's also a feeling of stillness, a deep penetrating silence, and I have the sense that I'm miles from anywhere. It's like landing in the middle of a slightly creepy Christmas card scene.

I wait impatiently with my arms wrapped around my ribs for warmth, knowing that my sister will appear at any second. But when she does, she's not alone, and the sight of the person walking beside her is so unexpected that it makes me stumble backwards until I'm sitting in a pile of snow.

/ /
Plain Sight

A group of volunteers are heading up the hill towards me. Two people linger at the back, fingers gently brushing, heads inclined towards each other in quiet conversation; my sister and Wren's brother. I stare at them like I've just seen a camel-train-mirage in the desert. None of the media reports from Millie's time as a volunteer ever mentioned a friendship between them, just the opposite in fact. Rumours were rife about conflicts and feuds within the group, and the feud that got the most publicity and attention was the one between Kit and Millie, the undisputed King and Queen of volunteers. Both of them were popular, camera-ready, confident and appealing. It was a shock to everyone, including me, when it became widely known that they clashed from their very first meeting.

I remember watching media clips that showed them arguing over shelter building in their training sessions. And the gossip that surrounded their first assignment together, where Kit was rumoured to have lost his temper and pushed Millie off a boat and into a saltwater lake. That was the reason why Kit abandoned my sister in the capture where they both died, because of the animosity between them, because they couldn't stand to be in the same room as each other, because of the clash between their headstrong personalities. But it's obvious that the two people walking towards me now have nothing but the deepest respect and affection for each other. They seem oblivious to their surroundings, enclosed in the bubble of their own private world, and I watch them with a growing feeling of confusion. Why has everyone been so misled about the relationship between my sister and Wren's brother?

Neither of them is the focus of this capture, I realise. They've simply walked into a site of special scientific or natural interest, one of thousands of areas across the globe where captures are taken to monitor changes in local conditions, where forest fires, landslides or avalanches pose a real danger. This conversation was overheard and captured by accident, as they passed through on their way to a different destination. And it's probably the only reason Millie could request it without raising any red flags.

I let them walk past me and then literally follow in the deep footprints they've left behind in the snow. As this capture is also set in observation mode, they will be totally unaware of my presence. The snow is so deep that I struggle to keep up. It's also difficult to catch every word of their conversation in the swirling wind that worries the treetops, and snatches their quiet exchange away from me.

"This is the craziest idea you've ever had," Kit says as they continue to trudge uphill. "We'll never get away with it, Millie, I can't believe you're even considering it." He looks around anxiously to make sure none of the other volunteers are eavesdropping. "Tobias Troy is already watching us far too closely, and if he keeps sending us into the kind of captures he's been picking out for us lately..."

Millie sighs wearily, and the difference between this Millie and the defiant Millie I saw in the last capture, just minutes ago, is so marked that it takes my breath away. She seems bitter and altered somehow.

"But it isn't crazy, and I've already done the most difficult part, so all we'd have to do is—"

"No!" Kit shakes his head, refusing to listen. "We've got to stick to our plan; it's the only thing that makes any sense. When we get to the end of our volunteering year—"

"*If* we get to the end of our year, you mean," Millie interrupts sulkily, folding her arms.

"Then nobody can tell us what to do anymore," Kit continues. His voice is softer now, encouraging, but there's also an unsettling undercurrent of desperation to his words. "We can save up some money, rent a flat in a leafy part of the city, you can get a place on that acting course, just like we've been talking about. We can't risk all of that for some ridiculous scheme that could get us both killed."

I get the sudden impression that they've had this conversation before, and that whatever Kit is trying to talk Millie out of, he won't succeed. Her stubborn streak was legendary. Nobody could make Millie do something if she didn't want to do it. Millie reaches out and grasps his gloved hand, squeezing it tightly, turning her head towards him. And that's when I catch a brief glimpse of her face.

Dark bruises disfigure her neck and cheeks with angry purple stains, injuries from another capture. I stare helplessly at the features of this angry girl and I barely see a trace of my sister. Not one news clip ever showed this version of Millie and the reasons for that are now plain. Three months of volunteering have transformed her. Millie is not the vivacious, fearless volunteer she was always portrayed as being. She's a furious, injured, sixteen year old girl who is way out of her depth. Almost every clip I've ever seen of her happily exploring flooded cave networks, or diving out of planes over remote islands in the Pacific, with a huge buzz of excitement, have been faked, I realise. The story of her volunteering life was a total fabrication.

I pull my hood back and vomit suddenly into the snow, the sight of my injured sister too harrowing to handle. While everyone, including me, thought she was enjoying the limelight, the fame and the glory of being a volunteer, the truth was far more disturbing. Did Scrim know, I wonder, wiping my mouth on my coat sleeve, breathing quickly from a shallow spot in my lungs. Did Millie tell her everything, or did she keep her silence to the very end, confiding only in Kit perhaps? I'm grateful that Kit and Millie had each other at the very least, that Millie wasn't alone.

By the time I've finished throwing up they've already disappeared over the top of the hill, the edge of the capture boundary, and there's nothing more to see. I race out of the booth and hit reload. This time, I get further up the hill. Joining the party ahead of Millie and Kit, I turn to watch as they walk towards me, hoping for another glimpse of my sister's face. But it's shrouded in the shadows of her deep hood, as if she'd already started to withdraw from the living world by the time this capture was taken, six weeks before her death. I could just walk up to her and lower the hood myself, Millie would notice nothing. But it feels wrong, like I'd be intruding on a private moment, so I keep my distance and let their little scene play out in full.

I play the capture all the way through several more times in a row, until my legs feel weak from the effort of ploughing through the snow, and I'm frozen to the bone. I listen to every word again and again, shocked each time by the fear in Kit's voice, and the close bond he'd already formed with Millie, the affection he felt for her obvious in his every movement. But it's impossible to work out what crazy scheme Millie was planning, or which part of it she'd already tackled by herself.

When I've finally had enough, I sit on the floor of the empty booth clutching my knees, head resting on the bony shelf they form, wondering if I can even face the final capture. But I know I have to do this for my sister, no matter how difficult. I have to understand the message she was trying to send me. I can't show these captures to anyone else, not even Hekla. This is up to me.

When I load the third capture a few minutes later, the screen outside the booth tells me exactly what I'm in for. *A Lesson at the Cromwell Street School Taken for the Social Archives. Status: Interactive Mode.*

My legs feel weak again, but this time from a feeling of sheer relief. Both me and Millie attended the Cromwell Street school between the ages of six and eleven years old. There are no nasty surprises waiting for me inside this capture. No special equipment is required either, except for maybe a pencil case. It's also set in interactive mode, which means that if I wanted to hug my sister, I could, and she would feel the warmth of my arms around her. If I wanted to talk to her, I could, pretending to be a new teaching assistant at the school, and she would answer any questions as if I'd asked them on the day the capture was taken. But it also means that if my teacher, Mrs Pennyfeather, was my sworn enemy, and I wanted revenge for the scolding she gave me, when I accidentally dropped a jar of green paint on Robin Nolan's desk, I could do anything I wanted to take that revenge. Many people have used captures for that very purpose.

Want to catch your boyfriend in the act of kissing the Prom Queen? Or come first against the cheat in the egg-and-spoon race at your school sports day? Or deliver the perfect put down to the bully who blighted your life? Everything is possible within the confines of a capture. But it's for this very reason that a code of behaviour was set forward by the Institute, in the very earliest years, demanding that the people in these captures should be treated with the same respect that all life deserves.

I've already decided not to speak to Millie; I couldn't bear to see any look of fear or alarm cross her face. But one thing puzzles me. Why, after letting me see what her life as a volunteer was truly like, does Millie now want me to go back in time, before any of this happened?

All traces of the damp snow smell vanish as the last capture emerges around me, and I'm suddenly standing in my old classroom at the Cromwell Street School. The air feels pleasantly warm after the snowy landscape. I remove my coat but keep my hat on to hide my hair, and then

I brush the familiar chalk-coloured walls with my fingers. It's like falling into a long lost memory. Every detail of this room was once so familiar to me I could trace all the cracks in the ancient ceiling, with my eyes closed, like country roads on a map. The desks are set in neat rows, all facing towards the teacher at the front, Mrs Pennyfeather, with her long black hair and a permanent ink stain on the third finger of her left hand. This could be my own memory instead of Millie's; everything is so unchanged and peaceful. I never thought I'd be here again.

I move carefully through the class as Mrs Pennyfeather scribbles on the blackboard, her back turned towards me, and study every face, recognising some from the grown-up versions I've seen at the Institute. I spot the back of Millie's head as I approach the front. She's sitting at the star pupil desk, bent over her exercise book, surrounded by colourful felt-tip pens, scribbling away with some concentration. She looks no older than nine or ten, fresh faced and already determined, her hair scooped back into two neat little braids. My real flesh and blood sister, caught exactly as she was at this moment in time, complete with a runny nose and a jam stain on the front of her blouse, the silvery tones in her hair so identical to mine.

I slide into the empty seat next to her and pretend to study the picture she's drawing. Her exercise book is covered in elaborate doodles and inky daydreams, unicorns, rainbows, a scene at the beach with buckets, spades and a happy family swimming in the sea. I pick up a pen from her collection and begin to add my own pictures, drawing castles and swirling clouds, just like I always used to when Millie allowed it. We sit side by side, sisters again, I'm aware of every soft noise she makes in concentration, of every idle swing of her foot, every blink of her eye. And I know exactly why she's chosen this particular capture for me to experience. This is how she used to be, how I remember her before the volunteering, happy, carefree and joyful in everything she did. I'm certain that she wants to remind me of who she really was. And I realise just how much I've missed her loud, warm, affectionate presence in the flat, which has always felt far too empty with just me, Yarena and Measles rattling around inside it, like a handful of dried peas at the bottom of a big glass jar. Millie is the missing piece of the puzzle, the essential ingredient that makes us whole. There's still a big Millie-shaped hollow in our home.

But there's something else as well, I notice as I study her doodles more closely. In her notebook, scattered among the unicorns and rainbows,

101

Millie has written the same three words, over and over, in different colours, underlined, surrounded by stars and fireworks. And it's these words that I am supposed to see, hidden in plain sight.

Spill. Hen. Mat.

The capture ends and just like the others I play it through several times more, watching carefully for anything I might have missed, relishing the chance to sit with my sister again. Then I exit the booth, reluctantly leaving the ghost of Millie behind, collect all three canisters and head down into the flat, which is still deserted and quiet. I make a hot chocolate, adding whipped cream and marshmallows; I've definitely earned some comfort food after everything I've just witnessed. Then I head straight for my room and lean back against the pillows on the bed, trying to understand the message Millie has just sent me, while everything is still clear in my mind. I've got no idea what the words in the last capture mean. I have a vague awareness that they come from a past that me and Millie shared. But the memory is so distant that the harder I try to pin it down, the more it seems to slip through my fingers, and the answer refuses to come.

I eventually give up and grab my laptop, which is sitting on the floor beside my bed, and type *Spill Hen Mat* into a search box. There are no results. The words are gibberish, even though there's something familiar about the arrangement of the letters, I can't see what any of it has to do with the other captures. I push my laptop aside wishing Millie had explained everything clearly in the note that she had delivered with the canisters. But how else could she be sure of convincing me that things weren't as they seemed? She had no idea that by now, I'd have firsthand experience of the way the Institute really works, that captures can be faked. She had no choice but to *show* me her reality. So I will have to figure this puzzle out for myself.

I only leave the flat when darkness falls and I realise how hungry I am. I take my laptop with me and head up to the cafeteria for more food, this time choosing some lasagne and garlic bread, followed by a large slice of apple pie and custard. I sit next to the window well away from everyone else, feeling out of sorts, my body clock confused by the rainforest rhythms. And I'm extremely glad I still have another two whole days before our next volunteering assignment. Just the thought of what might be waiting for us down in the sublevel booths is enough to make me grip my snow boots tightly, with my aching toes. Maybe Troy will go easy on us for once, and we'll be studying fish at an aquarium, or making daisy chains in a spring meadow. I'm already beginning to understand why some of those volunteers, who make it through their year, end up living reclusive lives in the remote Highlands of Scotland, where nothing can try to eat them, crush them, burn them or bury them.

I finally get back to the living quarters only to find another surprise, but this one is nowhere near as welcome as the message from Millie. Tobias Troy is pacing up and down the corridor, glaring at his watch, filling the space like an angry bear that's just been poked with a stick. After the difficult day I've already had, Troy is the last person I want to find anywhere near my door. But it's too late to turn tail and run. As soon as he sees me, Troy folds his arms and plants his feet firmly, blocking my doorway.

"Turn around, Yellabell, you're coming with me," he says, in the kind of voice that only a true psychopath could pull off, and it fills me with new dread. Has Troy somehow found out about the captures I've just seen? Can the Institute monitor what captures I've loaded into the private booth at home? Does he know that Millie is trying to send me a message, a message that involves him?

He strides back down the corridor, and I have no choice but to follow, feeling the safe pull of my room slowly slipping away behind me.

12
Training

Troy leads me up to the fourth floor without speaking another word, but I'm extremely relieved he's not heading for the sublevel capture booths. It's only as we pass the staff offices and head to the end of the corridor that I realise where he's taking me. He knocks on Aldora Scrim's door and then holds it open for me. I have to duck as I enter, just to avoid any contact with the damp underarm patches on his sweaty T-shirt. His stale body odour confirms everything I already think about him — tiny brain, massive ego, couldn't wash the stink of aggressive, pea-brained idiot off his body, even if he had a whole soap factory at his disposal.

He closes the door behind me and I move cautiously into the room. This time, however, there are no men sitting behind the desk, or women lurking in the shadows with clipboards. Scrim is the only occupant. She's dressed in a casual outfit, a thick grey jumper over loose-fitting black trousers. I can see the age lines on her face, the way her make-up collects in the creases around her eyes, like they've been softly highlighted with crayon. Maybe this isn't about the Millie captures after all...

"Kaida, I apologise for asking you up here during your time off, but I'm leaving for the Institute in New York in thirty minutes, and I wanted to talk to you first." She hurries round to my side of the desk, meeting me halfway across the room and hugging me firmly. I'm engulfed in a warm waft of her heavy vanilla scented perfume. I let my shoulders move away from my ears, just a little.

It feels like so long since I've been in the company of any adult who cares about my wellbeing, it's almost enough to make me crumble. But I manage to hold it together.

"How are you coping?" She stands back and checks me over for visible signs of injury, her eyes lingering on the lumpy bandage beneath my trouser leg, the cuts on my hands and my singed eyebrows.

"I'm still alive," I say, settling for the truth.

Scrim nods but there's no smile behind her eyes now. "I've been monitoring your volunteer assignments closely and I know it's been very tough. But you've shown a great deal of bravery and talent, just like your sister."

I know it's meant as a compliment, but now that I've seen the real volunteer Millie, with all her injuries, it's a little hard to swallow.

"I haven't forgotten about your allegations either," Scrim says, perching herself on the edge of the desk as we reach it, so our heads are at the same height. "I've been making some discreet enquiries. I've still got some close friends in the tech labs from when your father worked there, but it's very difficult to discover anything without asking some extremely difficult and potentially explosive questions."

"Do you think my dad knew something about the faked captures?" I ask, wondering if his highly secretive work involved watching over the other technicians in the sublevels.

But Scrim shakes her head. "Your father would have reported it straight to Cassian Cromwell himself if he'd ever suspected anyone of tampering." She sighs and pushes her fringe out of her eyes. "I wanted to ask you, Kaida, if you have any suspicions of your own, about who faked your capture."

What harm can it do to mention Troy? My situation is already precarious, and if Scrim can find some proof, and save Hekla the trouble of hacking into Troy's private accounts...

"I think it might be my team leader, Tobias Troy," I say, lowering my voice in case he's listening outside the door.

"Troy?" Scrim sounds surprised. "I know he can seem a bit unfriendly sometimes, and he's certainly one of the toughest team leaders we've got, but even so—" Her voice trails away. But the telltale look on her face suggests that she already has her own suspicions about him, and they might even match mine. "Do you have any evidence?"

"It's mostly just a feeling," I try to explain. "He keeps volunteering me for the most dangerous parts of our assignments and..."

"Yes?" Scrim urges as I consider my next words. Mentioning Hekla's theory about him eating puppies and kittens for breakfast won't help, I need something more concrete to tip the balance of this theory in my favour.

"And he seems to hate me for some reason, like he hated my guts before we ever met. I think he might have felt the same way about Millie too," I say, wondering if Scrim will pick up on the implication that mine might not be the only faked capture, that Troy could have been doing this for at least six years, sending countless volunteers to their fates.

Scrim folds her arms tightly and stands up, retreating behind her desk as if she needs the distance between us to consider my allegations.

"I will arrange to have you transferred to a different team, out of harm's way, out of Troy's way," she finally says. "I'll also make sure you're sent on some less challenging assignments, I think you've already experienced your fair share of danger."

I nod, grateful, not trusting myself to speak because of the sudden hope she offers, because my future might not be so bleak after all.

"Thank you," I eventually manage to say. "Could you get Wren transferred too?" I add, hoping the request isn't pushing my special privilege too far. "Troy's been singling him out as well."

"The McKenzie boy?" Scrim can't hide her obvious shock. But she keeps any opinions she might have on the subject to herself, and simply scribbles something on a notepad. "I will do everything I can, Kaida, but I can't make any promises. I would urge you again not to mention your suspicions to anyone until I have finished my investigations. This is extremely sensitive, the implications for Cassian Cromwell and the entire Institute if faking captures is even feasible, if Tobias Troy has been forcing people to volunteer..."

She breaks off with a brooding shake of her head, and for the first time I consider the impact this must be having on her. As principal of the college, the blame for everything that's been happening in the volunteer programme will land squarely on her shoulders. This has been weighing heavily on her too, I realise, but she has to see it through to the end now, neither of us has any choice.

She walks me back to the door and hugs me again, squeezing my shoulders one last time before finally letting me go. "Please stay safe, Kaida. If anything ever happened to you and I had to face Yarena..."

I nod, wishing it was a promise I could make with more confidence.

I head back to the living quarters alone, worn out by the day and every unexpected thing that's happened. I consider going to see Wren, he deserves to know the truth about his brother and my sister, but I decide to do it in the morning. I'm way too tired for that kind of conversation now. I need some solid sleep before I can handle anything else. So I stumble into my room, change into my pyjamas and collapse into bed. The charcoal grey cocoon is almost comforting and I let it soothe me into an exhausted, dreamless sleep.

A loud noise wakes me at 6.00 a.m. Someone is hammering on my door in a very unfriendly manner. I stagger out from under my duvet just to make the pounding stop. I fumble with the lock and then stand blinking into the hallway. It's only when my eyes adjust to the light levels that I see Troy. This is not a good way to start any day, especially as the acerbic expression on his face suggests he hasn't come to make peace. He takes in my tangled hair and the cuts, scratches and insect bites that are visible on my wrists and ankles, with something like a look of pleasure.

"You've got two minutes to get dressed."

He turns his back and I close the door, wondering if my visit to Scrim's office has already brought about change, if I'm being moved to another team. I pull on my clothes, or what's left of them, hop into my faithful boots instead of my volunteer's shoes, and attempt to drag a brush through my hair. Troy hammers on the door again and I yank it open, grabbing my jacket at the last minute. But instead of stopping to pick up Wren or any other volunteers for a new assignment, Troy marches me straight down to the sublevels on my own, past the entrance to the archives, the scene of my fake stealing spree.

"I thought Principal Scrim was transferring me to another team," I say cautiously, jogging along behind him with an awkward mix of half steps and stumbles.

Troy just smiles. "I have received no such request, Yellabell. It looks like you're stuck with me until I've finished with you."

His words make me shiver to the bone. "Then where are we going?"

"Training capture," is all Troy will say.

I catch sight of Wren a moment later. He's standing outside booth number twelve, looking puzzled. Troy must have woken him first.

"What's going on?" he asks as soon as he sees us heading towards him. The shaved spot on his head has already started to regrow and I'm reminded of a baby bird again.

"Because you've both shown such promise," Troy says with more than

107

a hint of sarcasm, as *promise* is not a word he's ever likely to use about either of us, "I've decided to put you through an advanced training capture. This particular capture is usually reserved for much more experienced volunteers, due to its difficult and challenging nature."

I instantly know we're in big trouble, if a training capture has to be played in the sublevels then it's bound to be treacherous. And if Troy has singled us out, with no other volunteers present, it means he doesn't want any witnesses. It also means he's been paying attention, he's noticed that me and Wren have formed a strange kind of friendship, and that we're now more like two awkward peas in a pod than age-old enemies. Or maybe he overheard my entire conversation with Scrim, who is now on her way to New York and powerless to help me. This thought makes me more fearful than anything else. Has Troy dragged me and Wren down to the sublevels *because* Scrim is now thousands of miles away, and on the wrong side of a deep ocean?

"But shouldn't you talk to Principal Scrim first, sir," I say, clutching at straws. "I mean, check if this capture is okay?"

"I do not take orders from Principal Scrim," Troy says abruptly, ending the conversation. He hurries us into the changing room area, which is cold and empty and clangs with the sound of our footsteps like the echoing chimes of doom. He loads a capture, waiting for the green light before opening the air locked door. "Wait in here for more instructions."

Wren shrugs and enters the capture first before I can even attempt to signal to him that this is a catastrophically bad idea. I follow reluctantly, expecting to find another rainforest, or a volcano or something even more volatile and unpredictable, a dragon maybe, waiting to breathe fire down upon us both. But instead we've entered through the back door of a truck, and the confined space is momentarily confusing. The truck is old-fashioned, military perhaps, the kind that gets used to transport medical supplies to the front line of a war zone, no windows, no other occupants. Troy closes the door behind us before we can bombard him with questions. We both take a seat on opposite sides, facing each other, there's nothing we can do now but wait it out.

"This is freaky," Wren says, surveying our unusual surroundings with more than a hint of apprehension. "I wonder where we're going." At that moment we hear an engine kick into life and the truck rumbles beneath us. "My money's on an experimental lab or another volcano," he adds, trying to lighten the mood, but it's not easy to smile when either of those options are a real possibility.

"If this is supposed to be a training capture, maybe they're taking us to some kind of camp in the desert?" I suggest, remembering Rilla's comment about Troy sending anyone he dislikes to the Australian Outback. I look more closely at the back of the truck but there's no equipment, no trace of sand or muddy footprints, and the terrain we're now travelling over feels rough and rocky. The door leading into the driver's cab is locked, I discover, when I gently try the handle.

"Where have you been for the last twenty-four hours anyway?" Wren asks, leaning forward and lowering his voice so it's barely audible. "I knocked on your door half a dozen times. I wanted to talk to you."

"Sorry, I went home for a while to use our old capture booth," I explain, clinging to the seat with my fingers as we go over a particularly large bump that flings us both sideways.

Wren raises a questioning eyebrow at me. "Not getting enough capture time down in the sublevels?"

I take a deep breath; I've already decided to tell him the truth so I plunge straight in. "It was the sixth anniversary of my sister's death." It was also the sixth anniversary of Kit's death, and Wren's features twist at the unnecessary reminder, but I need to explain this properly. "And Millie sent me some captures."

"I'm sorry, I shouldn't have joked about it," Wren says, looking flushed with embarrassment. "I thought you might be soaking up some sun on a beach, or visiting some ancient ruins in Greece, or whatever it is you find most relaxing." He pauses for a second. "What was it like, seeing Millie again?"

My throat tightens but I manage to keep the image of her bruised face at bay. "It was strange. I was only nine years old when she died, she looked different to the way I remember her."

"But she's the reason you volunteered?" Wren asks, and I can feel that it's more than just a casual question, he really wants to know. The noise in the truck is getting louder as we pick up speed. If ever there was a good time to tell him everything I've just discovered...if anyone is monitoring us at this moment, they'll have a hard time picking out my words above the low grinding of gears and the groaning of the engine.

I consider what I'm about to do for a few seconds before I lurch over to Wren's side of the truck and sit close beside him, our shoulders touching.

"I'm not here because of my sister," I say, as quietly as I can, ignoring the look of surprise on his face at my sudden nearness. "I already had a place on the captology course, but when they put me through my first solo capture, it was a fake."

Wren's expression hardens, the corners of his mouth bunching up into tight knots.

"You don't believe me?" I ask, wondering if I've just made a huge mistake. "You don't believe that captures can be faked?"

Wren looks directly at me but his face is now unreadable. "Tell me everything, Kaida," he says so quietly that I'm not sure if he's actually said the words, or if I've just imagined his response.

"The capture showed me going down into the archives, stealing three captures and taking them back home," I say hoping I'm doing the right thing by telling him. "When it finished, someone was waiting for me outside and they took me straight to Scrim's office."

Wren nods but says nothing, so I continue.

"Scrim told me I could either go to a detention centre for two years, or volunteer and then continue with my course next year, as if nothing had happened. I had no choice," I say, reliving the horrible moment on the day that my life changed forever. "Troy appeared with the canisters, the ones they said I'd stolen; he said they'd been found in my room."

"Let me guess, you never went anywhere near the archives?" Wren asks.

I shake my head. "The whole thing was a total fabrication, a complete set-up."

Wren thumbs his eyebrow, staring down at his feet, thinking hard, and he's just about to say something when the truck swerves to the left and we both topple sideways, like skittles in a bowling alley.

"Hey!" Wren yells, hauling himself up to his feet and hammering on the door of the driver's cab with his fists. "Watch where you're going, we're being thrown around in the back here!"

There's no answer, no sign that anyone has heard us over the roar of the engine. If anything, we seem to be speeding up, we're definitely heading downhill now, but there's still no clue about our destination, or what the training capture will involve when we get there. I sit down again and Wren eventually joins me still looking angry.

"So then yesterday," I continue without missing a beat, "three captures turned up in my room, they were requested by Millie five weeks before she died. And in one of them, I saw her and Kit together."

Wren turns so pale I wonder if the truck ride is making him travel-sick. But I carry on regardless.

"They seemed really friendly; they were talking quietly about their plans for a future together. They wanted to save up enough money to get their own place."

Wren just nods as if he accepts this alternative view of the relationship between our siblings without question. And that's when understanding finally dawns on me.

"You already knew they were close," I say.

Wren studies me anxiously, looking far more concerned about my reaction to this news than anything else. "I knew they weren't enemies, like the media always said. But who would have believed that, coming from me?"

I know he's right. Before the rainforest, if he'd tried to convince me that Kit and Millie had been close, I would have assumed it was all part of a cowardly plan to save his own skin.

"How did you know they were friends?" I ask, desperate for more information, for Wren's piece of the puzzle. "Did your brother send you captures too?"

Before he can answer, the truck swerves crazily to the left, catapulting us both forwards onto the floor. I land hard on my knees, pain shooting instantly through the bones and this time it's me who bangs on the door. But there's still no response.

"Do you reckon this is part of the training capture?" I ask, rubbing my kneecaps, which now feel like they're on fire.

"Being stuck with a maniac driver?" Wren frowns at the door.

"Maybe Troy's just trying to scare the pants off us both, seeing how long we'll put up with this before we hit the emergency stop button."

I scan the back wall of the truck where we entered the capture, but there's no sign of any button, emergency or otherwise. I try the door that separates us from the driver again, leaning into it with my full weight, but it's definitely locked.

"We should force it open," Wren says, reading my thoughts. "Before whoever's driving this truck crashes it into a brick wall."

He removes one of his boots, swaying with the motion of the truck, losing his balance several times before he manages to smash at the door and the handle with the heel. But it fails to make any impression.

"We need something heavier," he says.

There's nothing we can use in the back of the truck, everything is moulded into the body of the vehicle. But thanks to Grandma Hummingtree, and her desire to teach me everything she thought I might find useful in life, I know brute force isn't the only way to spring a lock. I check my pockets and find the two hairpins that I always keep handy.

Close up it's clear that the lock is old, rusty and corroded, so there's plenty of room for manoeuvre. I unbend one of the pins and wiggle it into the keyhole as a lever, and then use the second to push each of the locking pins up and out of the way; it takes me less than four minutes to defeat the door.

Wren shakes his head and stares. "Did your sister teach you how to do that?"

"Not my sister, my grandmother," I tell him, smiling when Wren looks simultaneously impressed and shocked.

We both pull on the door and yank hard until it finally flies open. Bright light hits us head-on through the large windscreen and I blink into the glare, until my eyes adjust to the sudden change. We're travelling down a steep dirt mountain track filled with potholes and rocks. And the reason for our uncomfortable journey is immediately obvious.

"There's no driver!" Wren says, holding onto the cab as we career downwards at an alarming speed.

The driver's cab is completely empty. It's a miracle we haven't already plunged over the side of the mountain, but the wheels seem to be following a deep groove in the road, swinging round the tight bends like the truck's mounted on rails. Only our luck can't last forever.

"Please tell me you know how to spring locks *and* drive trucks?" Wren says.

"I only know the basics." I'm already staggering over to the driver's seat, quickly trying to remember the lessons Grandma Hummingtree gave me, but this is nothing like driving an old tractor around the scattered barns and outbuildings at the farm in Northumberland. I lower myself into the seat, grasp the steering wheel with nervous sticky hands, slam my foot down hard on one of the pedals and we speed up instantly.

"Whoa, wrong peddle!" Wren shouts as I remove my foot quickly and try the one next to it, which should be the brakes.

"Nothing's happening!" I pump the peddle hard, my leg straightening out to its full stretch, my back arched away from the seat with the effort. "The brakes don't work!"

I grab the handbrake instead and yank it back, there's a low grinding sound, the truck stutters for a second and then continues hurtling down the mountain at the same terrifying speed. "The handbrake's been disabled too. Here, take the steering wheel, I need to check something at the back of the truck."

Wren attempts to guide us round the next series of death-defying bends. I stumble into the back again and try the doors, but Troy has locked them from the outside, and my hairpin trick doesn't work a second time round. We're trapped like bugs in an upturned jar.

"The back doors are locked and I can't open them!" I tell Wren as I join him again in the driver's cab.

"Troy locked us in here? Why didn't he just shove us straight over the edge of a cliff and be done with it?"

We swap places again and Wren transfers himself to the seat beside me. "Can't you turn off the engine? It might slow us down at least."

I lean over the steering wheel and fumble around for the ignition without taking my eyes off the road.

"No keys," I say. "Somebody wanted to make absolutely sure we didn't get out of this capture alive. We could jump," I suggest, looking out of Wren's window as the bare rock of the mountain races past at a dizzying speed. "We might survive if we time it right."

But we both know the chances are slim and there's still no guarantee we'd live long enough to be found and rescued.

I hold on tight, feet braced against the floor as we fly round two sharp hairpin curves. This time the truck sways violently to the right and I only just manage to keep it on the track. The sheer drop on my side is enough to smash anything that strays over the edge into very tiny pieces.

"This definitely isn't a training capture," Wren says. "It's a notorious experiment from the early years, I remember reading about it. The Institute did a whole series of deadly captures and then put people inside them to see what would happen, to see if they would actually die."

There's no doubt about the bad ending that's coming our way, and soon. The next sequence of spaghetti hoop bends looks even tighter than the last, and the truck is now travelling at breakneck speed.

"Listen, Kaida, I've got to tell you why I'm here," Wren says, tearing his eyes away from the road and focusing on me. "It's not what you think, I volunteered for a reason."

But before Wren can explain any more, the truck finally parts ways with the road, the angle of the bend too severe for the wheels to stick to, and we sail over the edge. For a moment I feel as weightless as an eagle's feather floating down from a treetop nest, and there's a strange stillness all around us like a big pause in the universe, a silent gasp of shock. All I can see ahead of us is sky, blue and perfect, and the tension in my body unexpectedly disappears. This is not how I thought I would die. Some part of me believed I'd make it through my year of volunteering, against all the impossible odds. And even though I'm now sitting in a flightless bird of a truck, I still can't quite let go of the idea of living.

I stare at Wren, who looks equally shocked at finding himself on the very edge of death, and then we're plummeting and I know we've got just seconds left to breathe, to feel, to exist. There's no room to feel any fear. I grip the inside of my faithful old boots with my toes and reach out, grabbing Wren's hand, thinking of Yarena and Measles, hoping I'm about to see Millie, Mum and Dad again. I've even got time to wonder if that's how it really works. Will I meet with them in a landscape of fluffy, swirling clouds and angels?

An odd whining noise breaks through into the cab. There's a sudden change around us, a jarring shift as the sky disappears and everything goes dark, but the impact I'm expecting doesn't come. Instead, the driver's cab melts away and we're still falling but more slowly now, my arms and legs suddenly unsupported and floundering. I lose my grip on Wren's hand, we crash to the ground side by side, dazed, but definitely one hundred percent still in the land of the living. I'm facing the floor of the booth; someone has pulled the capture at the very last second, dissolving the velocity that we carried over the edge of the mountain with us, and saving us from certain oblivion.

Wren's face is so pale with shock and disorientation that he looks like a Hollywood version of the ghost he almost became. There's noise around us now, people running to the spot where we've landed.

114

"What the hell are you two doing in here without permission?"

Our trainer, Cyrus Roth, is looming over us, but he's forced to one side as a whole team of medics descend and begin to check us over.

"You were five seconds away from being dead. That capture was banned more than a century ago! If someone hadn't noticed that this booth was in use, if they hadn't taken the time to check which capture was being played..." Roth pauses, regrouping, checking his anger. "Where did you get it? Who gave it to you?"

His questions go unanswered, swallowed up by the swarm of people now buzzing around us. I get one last look at his face, puce with rage, as we're both carried towards the exit. But I already know neither me nor Wren will mention Troy's name, when it comes to the questions that will inevitably follow. Now that the capture has failed to do its job and kill us, he will definitely try again, but convincing anyone other than Scrim of his intentions will be an impossible task. Troy could deny our accusations with a hundred different plausible explanations. But that's not what occupies my thoughts as we're whisked away from the sublevels.

In the final seconds, when we were plunging towards certain death, I suddenly thought of the three little words scrawled across Millie's notebook, and I remembered what they meant. And now that I'm not dead, I know exactly what to do with them.

13
BMLC

I spend the next nine hours in hospital being x-rayed, stuck with needles and checked over thoroughly for hidden internal injuries. But the only thing I'm suffering from is bruised knees, which now look like two stormy skies on a thunder-filled evening. Wren is kept well away from me at the other end of the hospital; Roth spends twenty minutes grilling me about how we ended up in a capture that almost killed us. I tell him that we thought it was just a normal training capture, available to all volunteers, and that there must have been some sort of mistake in the archives, no mention of Troy or the fact that he locked us inside the truck to seal our fate.

By the end of the day, everyone's treating it as an unfortunate mix up, even Troy has the gall to show his face and act all concerned for my welfare, in front of Roth. Scrim has now arrived at the New York Institute, according to the newsfeed that plays in the hospital. So there's no way I can tell her what's happened, how Troy has tried to kill me and Wren, for that I need a face-to-face conversation, if I ever get another chance. It's too risky to tell anyone else the truth in case word gets back to Troy, making him even more determined to wipe us off the face of the volunteering world. For now, we have to go along with the pretence that it was all an accident and take our punishment, whenever Roth decides to dispense it, for being 'dim-witted, idiotic, moron brains.'

I'm finally allowed to return to the living quarters, accompanied by a stern-faced Roth, who sees me right to the door of my room, in case I somehow manage to find fresh danger between the hospital bed and the Institute. When I open the door a blurry shape rushes towards me and pulls me into a bone-crushing hug.

"I tried to see you in the hospital but they wouldn't allow any visitors," Yarena says, her voice hoarse with worry, her hair falling out of its usual neat bun. She holds onto me for what feels like an hour, and then studies me at arm's length to inspect the damage.

"I'm fine," I say, with a traitor quiver in my voice, because her unexpected visit has pierced a hole in my flimsy armour.

She nods and swallows hard. "I just wanted to see for myself."

"And Aldora Scrim's putting me on a different team," I tell her, hoping more than ever that Scrim will keep her promise.

Yarena frowns. "Aldora told you that in person?"

"She called me up to her office yesterday to see how I was doing." And to discuss the problem of faked captures but I decide not to mention that. Why add to Yarena's worries when nothing has been resolved yet. The meeting with Scrim already seems like days ago, and my head aches whenever I think about it.

Yarena only leaves when she's straightened up the clothes that I've flung around my room, remade my bed, and fussed over whether I'm getting enough to eat, whether I need another batch of cakes to keep me going. She doesn't even bother trying to convince me that I should ask to be dropped from the volunteering programme. All her hopes now rest on Scrim's promise. I lock the door, change into a comfy top and sweats, grab my laptop and sit on my bed leaning back against the wall. I've already been fed in the hospital. I've had hours to slowly let my body deal with the shock of the terrifying truck ride, and several shots of pain medication which have left me with a strange, floating, out-of-body sensation. But I feel as normal as it's reasonable to feel after the dramatic day I've just had. And I'm now itching to try and unravel Millie's secret message.

As me and Wren were careering towards certain annihilation, my memory finally delivered me with the answer I've been searching for, and I now realise why it was so hard to remember. *Spill Hen Mat* is an anagram of Millie's favourite made-up word, *smelliphant*. As far back as I can remember she used it to describe everything from her mood, to her favourite food and her best friends. Buried for years beneath a weight of sorrow and sadness, the memory had stubbornly refused to resurface until the threat of imminent death. Only then had some part of me lifted all subconscious restrictions and taboos I'd placed around it.

Millie also said it every time she called me on LondonCall from her room, just before bedtime, our secret goodnight ritual that continued until the day she volunteered. I type the word into the search box on my LondonCall account now, but it shows nothing. I bring up Millie's account instead, it's still part of the family account we all share with Grandma and Grandpa Hummingtree. Millie's account is marked as dormant, not deceased, which means there is unfinished business. I feel my heart quicken as a password box appears and I type in *smelliphant*, being careful to hit the right keys. After several agonising seconds the account opens and there's one recorded message, unopened, sent six years ago, exactly two weeks before she died. This is what I was supposed to find.

I'll only be able to see it once, messages cannot be saved and after so many years, there's a good chance I won't be able to play it again either. I've got one shot at taking it all in. I breathe deeply, trying to lower my heart rate, then I tap the message and it opens on my screen. Millie is looking straight into the camera, dressed in the same style of volunteer clothes that I have spent the last weeks wearing. She's sitting in a room that could be the very one I now occupy, with its soulless charcoal walls. The unnerving thought sends a deep chill through me, this is the last LondonCall message she ever sent.

"Hey Little Dragon." Her voice sounds husky with tiredness and suppressed emotion. She looks scared, thin-faced and hollow, but it's still so good to hear her speak directly to me, like she's alive again for just a few precious moments. "There's a special place under The Lid where people hide things," she says with no introduction, her assumption being that if I've got this far, I know I'm looking for something. "Find the angel's wings and the drops of blood." There's a sudden knock on the door, and for a moment I'm not sure whether the sound is coming from my door, here in the present, or her door, six years ago. But Millie looks over her shoulder with a startled, frightened expression and with one lingering look, the brief message ends. A notice appears telling me that this LondonCall account is now deceased. It shuts down automatically leaving me with a blank screen. But I play the message over again inside my head, closing my eyes, picturing the haunted look on her face, like she knew the knock on the door signalled the beginning of the end. I'll never be able to forget that look. I add it willingly to my treasured store of Millie memories. I don't discriminate. Good or bad, a memory is a memory.

I spend the next ten minutes wondering what she could have hidden under The Lid and why it's so important. Then I message Hekla, asking her to meet me tomorrow morning at 7.00 a.m. She's the only person who will know where we can find the angel's wings and the drops of blood. But it's too late to visit her now and I have to tell her about Millie's message face-to-face, away from the Institute, before Troy can turn up at my door and attempt to finish what he's already started.

There's one last thing I have to do. I close my laptop, pull on my slippers and head down the corridor, turning right, knocking softly on a door identical to mine. Wren opens it cautiously, his face relaxing into a tired smile when he sees me.

"Oh, it's you."

Strictly speaking, we're not allowed to be alone together in each other's rooms, but nothing is going to stop me from getting to the truth of Wren's story. He offers his unmade bed for me to sit on as he swiftly checks that nobody has seen me enter, and then he closes the door. His room is just like mine, except for a row of leafy green plants on the windowsill that are clearly flourishing under Wren's care, and they give the space a feeling of serenity and homeliness that mine still lacks. His clothes are heaped over the back of a chair, his shoes scattered across the floor like they've been searching for his feet. He's just as messy as I am; the thought makes me smile.

"Roth told me to stay in my room, but I was just on my way to see you," Wrens says, and I notice he's only wearing one sock. The other sock is rolled up in his hand. "Are you okay? Roth yelled at me every time I asked him."

I show him my bruised knees then curl my legs up beneath me as I settle myself on his bed. "Troy came to see me when I was alone."

"You're honoured; all I got was a bunch of very insistent doctors who kept trying to give me sedatives. What did Troy say?"

"That we'd been given the wrong capture and he didn't realise."

"So he didn't realise when he was locking us inside the truck?"

"Or when we were hammering on the door trying to get out. Are you injured?" I ask, noticing a bandage on his wrist.

"It's just a graze," he says, dismissing the injury quickly. "Considering we could have been lying in a morgue right now, I'm not complaining. I really thought we were going to die this time." His voice breaks on the final word and he struggles to keep it together in front of me, clenching his jaw.

I know exactly how he feels and I have to scrunch up both my fists, trying to stop the tremor in my hands. I'm in big trouble if it ever travels over the rest of my body and reaches my vital organs. "You were going to tell me why you volunteered," I say, when we're both calm and quiet again, "in the truck, before we went over the edge, you said you had to tell me something."

Wren sits on the floor, arms resting on his bent knees, as he fiddles with his bandage. But I can tell he's just trying to work out where to begin his story, so I wait patiently until he's ready. This is something he was only prepared to share with me when all hope was lost. So whatever it is, he deserves some space to figure it out. And it's nice, just sitting together without some new threat to life careering towards us. It feels kind of normal, like something two old friends would do on an ordinary Wednesday evening, or whatever day it is now. I lost track long ago.

"When I was nine years old, my brother left his course at university to become a volunteer," Wren says quietly, and even the plants on the windowsill seem to be turning their leaves away from the light, listening to his story. "It was a total shock to the whole family; he'd never shown any interest in captures or becoming a volunteer. But my dad says he suddenly showed up one weekend, announcing that he'd got bored with studying physics, and that he'd already signed an agreement. He was determined and nothing they said could stop him." Wren pauses considering his words carefully before he continues. "Four months later, he died in the same volunteer disaster as your sister. It was pretty rough going for a few years, my mum and dad never forgave themselves for letting him leave his course. It was terrible hearing what everyone else thought of my big, stupid, loveable brother, and how he'd callously abandoned Millie to her death. The media hounded my parents, implying that it was somehow their fault, that the death of their son wasn't enough to deal with, they had to be blamed for Millie's death as well." Wren glances anxiously at my face, gauging my reaction, but I'm careful not to show any kind of emotion. "None of us could believe for a second that Kit would ever abandon anyone, he couldn't even walk past a garden worm without picking it up and putting it somewhere nice and earthy. But we were confronted with the evidence again and again. The capture showed us that he was a coward, that he let his dislike of Millie influence his behaviour in the worst possible way. And yet how could we accept that any of it was true?"

For the first time I truly understand what Wren and his family must have been through and it's impossible not to feel his pain. I wrap my arms around my middle trying to stop the sudden aching pains that the dreadful realisation causes.

"And then, three months ago, I was sorting through some of my old stuff in the attic, Mum wanted us all to have a big clear-out, and I came across a box of Kit's possessions," he says. "Someone at the Institute had gathered up everything from his room, after his death, and sent it to my parents. It didn't contain much, just some spare volunteer clothes, a book he'd been reading about physics and an old pair of shoes. But whoever gathered up his stuff obviously hadn't bothered checking very thoroughly, because Kit had stuffed a note inside one of his shoes describing how he'd been set-up."

I clutch my middle even harder as Wren takes a note from his pocket. The sheet of paper is water stained with one serrated edge, as if it was torn hastily from a notebook. The fold lines have deepened with age, giving the note an ancient look, like an important historical document.

"Kit describes how two men turned up at his university, out of the blue, and escorted him to London," Wren says, opening the note out so he can read his brother's words. "Scrim showed him a capture where he'd supposedly been caught destroying a collection of very old captures, a series of famous lectures given by eminent physicists, on loan to the university. It was completely faked, of course, but my brother had no choice, Scrim told him to volunteer, or go to jail, just like she did with you, Kaida."

The certain knowledge that mine and Millie's were not the only captures to be faked isn't much comfort. Wren shows me the note as proof, and I read it slowly, taking in every detail. Kit's handwriting is small and neat, but towards the bottom it becomes more erratic and sprawling, a reflection of his troubled state of mind. The final two sentences are short but they make the biggest impression on me. *Millie Hummingtree knows everything. If I die, find her and help her.*

"Did you show your parents the note?" I ask, feeling desperately sad for Wren's family and the wretched years of torture they've endured.

Wren shakes his head. "I couldn't, everyone still hates them so much, if they'd gone to the media, or even to Scrim or Cassian Cromwell, claiming that Kit had been set-up, no one would have believed them. But I couldn't just carry on with my own life as if nothing had changed," Wren says with a shoulder shrug. "That's why I volunteered. My parents went totally berserk, but I have to find out what's really going on, Kaida, why Kit and Millie really died, we both do." He stands up suddenly and perches on the edge of the bed, too agitated to sit on the floor any longer. "I mean, if someone's faking captures, then maybe we can prove that Kit didn't really abandon your sister at the end. You said you saw them together?"

I nod. "They were really close, Wren. It wasn't like everyone thought, Millie was angry and bruised and Kit was trying to talk her out of some crazy idea she'd had. I don't believe he left her to die. He wouldn't have done that."

Wren nods, clenching his jaw again, struggling to keep whatever he's feeling under tight control. "This changes everything," he says. And I know he's right. Me and Wren now share a very different family history. We can both feel the instant shift, a strengthening of the bond we've already formed. It's as if we were always meant to uncover the truth, as if truth was the magnetic force that brought us together in the first place. And just like magnets, it will now take something much more powerful to pull us apart.

It's also a relief to talk about it. Other than a few snatched moments with Hekla, I've had to keep every suspicion locked away inside myself, with no one to tell me if I'm on the right track or as crazy as a March Hare. I tell him about Hekla's discovery that under Troy's team leadership the number of volunteers has doubled.

"Do you really think this is just about recruiting enough volunteers?" Wren says, thoughtfully, playing with his bandage again.

"Do you have another idea?"

Without hesitation, he shoots to his feet, takes something from a drawer beside his bed and hands it to me. It's one of the glass vials we use for storing samples during our volunteering assignments, and inside it sits a scrap of yellow plastic bearing the letters *BMLC*.

"Brimstone Mining and Logging Corporation," Wrens says, as I inspect it, puzzled.

BMLC are so huge that practically everyone has heard of them. They sponsor loads of major sporting events and their head office, a brutal concrete oblong of a building, which everyone calls The Coffin, is located right here in London, overlooking the Thames.

"What do you know about volcanoes, Kaida?"

I frown, thrown by the sudden change of subject but I play along. "I know you should never get too close to one that suddenly starts spewing out smoke and fumes."

Wren automatically thumbs his singed eyebrows. "But did you also know that when magma rises from deep inside the earth, it brings up a whole load of minerals with it, things like tin, silver, gold and diamonds, which then get caught inside volcanic rocks? Eruptions also churn out loads of sulphur deposits, and sulphur is used to bleach sugar, and make things like matches and fertiliser, and to vulcanise rubber."

"So you found this during our first capture assignment in the volcano?" I ask, turning the vial over again.

Wren nods. "I think it comes from a safety vest, or a sample bag."

And I suddenly understand what he's implying. "You think BMLC are paying Troy to explore captures for them?"

"Brimstone is supposed to discover new deposits using robots and drones, according to their friendly, shiny website," Wren says with a cynical looking smile. "But nothing beats the dexterity of a human hand when it comes to taking samples from difficult places, or in harsh environments where drones and robots are prone to mechanical faults and sudden failures."

"That explains why we had to collect so many rock samples," I say, remembering how baffled I was at the time. "And what does it matter if a few volunteers die along the way? Troy said as much to me after I pulled you out of the crater."

"And if things go wrong, you can always cover up the truth with a faked capture."

"So that's why he really took us into the rainforest," I add, realising that our worksheets had nothing to do with conservation or observation. "BMLC make money from logging hardwood trees too."

It goes against Cassian Cromwell's most important founding principle, no captures for money. But Wren has clearly given this a lot of thought, and I can think of no other reason why a group of volunteers would be sent to explore the crater of a volcano. Especially if that volcano belonged to BMLC, and I'm holding the evidence which proves that it did, in my hands. How else could a scrap of yellow plastic, bearing their company name, have ended up inside the crater of a volcano? The chances of it being blown there by itself, on the east wind, or being accidentally dropped from cruising height by a passing albatross are laughable.

I study the scrap of yellow plastic in the vial. Wren's theory explains everything perfectly, except for why Troy has been trying to kill us both with such villainous enthusiasm.

"Have you told anyone else your theory, any of your friends?" I ask.

Wren shakes his head and smiles sadly. "I'm looking at the only friend I've had since the age of nine, I wasn't exactly popular at school."

We're both silent for several moments as Wren's confession lingers in the room, and I realise that the plants on the windowsill are there for more than just decoration, they're his faithful companions too. Just like me and my boots, they offer him a sense of comfort and belonging, and I understand better than anyone how strongly he feels about them. I wait until I have his full attention again before delivering my final piece of information.

"Millie left me a secret message on LondonCall," I say slowly, letting my words sink in. "She told me about a place under The Lid where people hide things, but she got cut off before she could tell me anything else. I'm going to find it for myself tomorrow morning. I think you should come with me."

The clouds finally lift from Wren's face.

"What time are we leaving?"

14
Dark

Sleep doesn't come easily after the day I've just had and my troubled dreams are filled with bruised snowy landscapes, and my sister's haunted face on the last LondonCall message she ever sent.

I wake in the early hours convinced I can feel Millie sitting on the end of my bed, until I slowly remember that she's not real, just another night time apparition. But I lean against the apparition, and imagine that Millie is telling me great long fanciful tales about fearsome pirates, just like she always used to when a thunderstorm woke me in the night, and I couldn't sleep from a childhood terror of where the lightning might strike next.

I get up early the next morning and tread softly down the corridor, carrying my boots so I won't wake any of the other volunteers. Wren is already waiting for me outside his room, looking grey-skinned and tired, and I wonder if he's been visited by his own night time phantoms. We hurry through the cafeteria, grabbing hot buns and banana milk for breakfast on the fly, and head up to the rooftop garden, catching the first gondola to Mole Valley. The gondola is deserted; we sit on opposite sides of the carriage and watch the grand old buildings of London slide beneath us as we travel through grey morning mist. It's beautiful at this early hour, with a stillness broken only by soaring families of magpies, scavenging for food between the rooftop gardens.

Hekla meets us inside the gondola station dressed in red jeans and a pea-green coat, and I wonder if I should have asked her to wear something a little less conspicuous. Her face passes through all the stages of anger and confusion, in rapid succession, as she recognises Wren.

"What the hell's he doing here?" She backs away from him, the brother of the volunteering coward that she has despised, along with everyone else, for the last six years.

"His brother got volunteered with a fake capture too," I say quietly.

"So? That doesn't change the fact that he left your sister to die."

Her words make me wince. I take Hekla forcefully by the arm, before she can cause a scene and draw unwanted attention to us. I walk her away from Wren and over to a quiet corner next to a broken ticket machine, quickly explaining the captures I've seen, the truths I've uncovered, Wren's discovery in the volcano and how it all ties in with BMLC. It's a lot to believe and accept. I have to tell her the whole story twice before her face begins to soften just a little. And I know it will take Hekla some time to deconstruct the layers of hate she's built up over the years around the whole McKenzie family. But by the time we rejoin Wren thirty minutes later, she swears she's willing to take my word for it that he can be trusted. Although the guarded look in her eyes tells a different version of that story.

"So why did you want to meet me, Little Dragon?" Hekla asks. Her gaze stays fixed on Wren, re-evaluating, trying to decide if I've somehow been hoodwinked by his story. Wren blinks at her benignly, like he's considering the idea of befriending a nervous fox.

"Millie left me a message on LondonCall. She said there's a special place under The Lid where people hide things. She told me to find the angel's wings and the drops of blood."

Hekla's whole attention is suddenly focused on me. "Millie hid something in the Wall of the Dead?"

"Can you take us there?" Wren asks, tentatively, maintaining a safe distance from Hekla, who still looks like she could turn feral at the slightest provocation.

"Of course I can." She pauses, folding her arms so tightly across her chest that her knuckles blanch. "Is this your first time under The Lid?"

Wren nods.

"Then you'd better watch out for falling slabs of rock. Only three people have been killed this month, so we're probably safe. But if you hear anyone yelling, don't stop to ask any stupid questions, just run."

It's an old Moler's tease. No one has ever been killed by falling rock, but Hekla delivers the line with such a serious face that when we step out of the gondola station, I notice Wren checking the slab above our heads every few seconds.

On the weekend, the subterranean levels are even more oppressive, the streets already beginning to fill with people and it somehow makes the space feel doubly claustrophobic. I have to concentrate on my feet as we walk, just to stop any kind of panic from setting in. Hekla veers quickly off the main road and leads us through a maze of narrow lanes, where all the traders have spilled out onto the streets. We're quickly engulfed in a confusion of garish lights and brightly coloured displays of glass beads, stripy jumpers and painted crockery. Conversation is impossible above the short blasts of loud music coming through every open doorway, and when we finally reach the end of the lanes my clothes stink of hot dogs and cheap patchouli oil. Hekla dives down an alleyway which opens out into a large cobbled square with benches, burger vans and flowerbeds full of artificial roses that look just a little too red.

"This is Dead End Square," she informs us, and the reason for its name is strikingly obvious. At the far side of the cobbles stands a wall of solid bedrock, stretching all the way up to The Lid. We've reached the eastern most boundary wall of the subterranean levels.

"This place feels like a tomb," Wren says quietly, as we approach the Wall of the Dead for a closer inspection.

Over the years it's been heavily graffitied so that more than ninety percent of the rock is now covered in spray-painted hearts, personal messages and nicknames, written in every colour of the rainbow. Striking images of London, Mole Valley and famous cartoon characters sit happily alongside some larger-scale works of art, that wouldn't look out of place in a gallery. A grid of narrow wooden steps has been anchored to the face of the wall with bolts, sideways-on, allowing access to the upper reaches for the brave. The sheer scale of it is intimidating. It's only when we get up close enough to touch it that I notice hundreds of holes, gouged into the rock.

"People come here and leave offerings, treasures, notes to the dead," Hekla explains. She removes a chunk of rock from a hole the size of her fist, and shows us a dried flower and a string of glass beads that have been lovingly arranged inside. "Since we're already buried underground, I guess it's the closest thing we've got to a shrine."

"Maybe that's why there are so many pairs of angel's wings," Wren says, taking three steps back and peering upwards.

My heart sinks. Angel's wings account for at least a third of the graffiti; they appear in all shapes and sizes and come in every shade of white and gold imaginable. They're beautiful too and completely overwhelming.

"This is going to be harder to find than a lullaby in a pillow factory,"

Hekla says, hands braced behind her head, studying the full height of the wall.

"We'd better split up so we can cover more ground," Wren suggests.

Hekla scampers upwards, this clearly isn't the first time she's scaled the rock. Wren takes a different more cautious route, leaving me to investigate the wings that sprout up from the base of the wall. It's impossible not to get lost in the beautiful designs, some with actual feathers, and the details of the stories they protect. But none have drops of blood or messages from Millie, and I'm forced to pick a set of steps that head up the face of the wall. Compared to the captures that me and Wren have already been through, it's a walk in the park, but I'm careful not to glance down at the ground in case I lose my nerve. Now would not be a good time to discover I'm afraid of angels, or walls.

The higher up the rock I go, the more personal the graffiti becomes. Faces have been etched into the upper reaches and like ghostly guardians, they watch as I search. Their presence is so unnerving that I almost miss the drops of blood when I eventually find them. Somebody has tried to hijack the image, turning the drops into cherries with spindly green stalks. But enough of the original painting survives for me to see the blood cascading down over a tiny, delicate, pair of feathered wings. After six years of new graffiti, I know we're lucky that Millie's message is still visible, and I touch the wall in silent thanks. There's just one problem. Millie was always several inches taller than me, at every age, and there's no way I can reach the hole that sits underneath the wings.

"Found something?" The voice behind me is Wren's.

I show him the blood and the wings and demonstrate the shortfall in the length of my arms. Wren's not much taller than me. So our only option is to work together. I try to summon up all the courage of Grandma Hummingtree and my stilt-walking mum as Wren holds onto the back of my jeans, and I lean out from the steps, extending my arms. The toes of my right foot are pressed hard against the wall so I don't slip and tumble fifty feet to a broken neck. Not even Wren can hold my entire weight if I suddenly fall.

"Kaida, you're leaning out too far," he warns, and I feel him trying to yank me backwards, to reel me in.

But I'm so close I have to swallow my rising panic and try just a little bit harder, practically unhinging my shoulder from its socket, stretching out the last impossible inch. My fingers claw at the wall. "I can almost reach it!" When I loosen the rock under the wings, it slips through my fingers and falls to the ground. I hear Wren swearing under his breath as I search inside the hole, testing his grip on my jeans to the absolute limit.

The only thing it contains is a plain wooden box, bone-dry and protected from ageing by the sterile environment of the wall. I have to use both hands to remove it from its hiding place. Wren finally heaves me back to the safety of the steps, still holding onto me in case I decide to climb again.

"Don't ever do that again!" he says, white faced with fear. "I'm serious, I almost dropped you. You could have been a big ugly splatter on the ground by now."

"Sorry," I say, feeling my face burn, adjusting my jeans so they sit properly on me again.

But Wren doesn't hold a grudge, and he shakes his head with the first hint of forgiveness. "Are you sure you're not a genuine volunteer, because you're starting to act like a natural."

I have to lean against the wall for several minutes until my legs have stopped shaking, then we head back down to ground level, signalling to Hekla. We find a place to sit on some artificial grass, under an oak tree that has its own daylight hood for growth. And that's when the real nerves kick in. After the convoluted trail that has led me here, I'm suddenly worried about what the contents of the box might reveal. Am I ready to see what Millie left behind? I stare at the box for so long that Hekla finally punches me playfully in the arm.

"Do you want me to open it?" she offers.

I shake my head and slowly lift the lid. Part of me has been expecting to find more evidence that Kit and Millie were together, or at least a letter written in Millie's erratic scrawl. The one thing I truly wasn't expecting to discover was another capture. The black beetle shine of the canister is so familiar it takes me a second to register how serious this is. And it's not the only troubling thing the box contains. There's also a capture machine, easily recognisable from its clear glass eyes and the brass stamp on the side declaring it's the property of *The Cromwell Institute of Captured Time*. But before I can even think about picking it up, Hekla snatches the whole box out of my hands and snaps it shut; the sound echoes around us like a whip snap.

"We can't look at this here." She's already on her feet with the box parcelled possessively under her arm. She heads back across the cobbled square, leaving me and a puzzled looking Wren with no choice but to follow.

It takes twice as long to retrace our route through the lanes now that more people have poured out onto the congested streets, and there's no question of any explanation from Hekla. But I know she must have a solid reason for her actions. She's only ever this silent when something is seriously wrong. She takes us back to her flat on Gaskell Road; it's totally deserted and seems unnaturally quiet without the different strains of clashing music that usually greet anyone who enters.

"Everyone's out," Hekla explains as she shoots up the stairs and straight into her bedroom.

I'm so happy to be back in the familiar, reassuring surroundings that I feel myself relax just a little, despite the very sombre reasons that have brought us here. But Wren pauses in the doorway and gazes at the chaos of her room, like a visitor at a natural history museum observing the habitat of a rare and strange creature. "How do you ever find anything in here?" he asks.

Hekla's eyes narrow, she refuses to dignify his remark with a verbal response. But I know she'll be storing up her answer for later, and I wonder if I should warn Wren that he could be in seriously deep water.

Hekla clears a space on her floor, flinging shoes, books and magazines aside until there's room for all three of us to sit in a circle, like witches gathered around a cauldron.

"So why all the drama?" Wren asks.

Hekla opens the box and removes the contents with a delicate touch, like a conservator handling some ancient Roman pottery or an Egyptian mummy at a museum.

"This is a genuine dark capture," she tells us, placing it on the carpet with reverence. "Which means it's unofficial and highly illegal. Just sitting in the same room with this capture is enough to get all three of us incarcerated for a minimum of fifteen years."

I'm not sure I've ever truly believed in the existence of dark captures until this moment. Wren touches the canister carefully with the tip of his middle finger and then pulls away, as if the mere presence of the capture is enough to burn him with guilt.

"How can you tell it's a dark capture?" I ask, studying it closely, because it looks like every other capture I've ever seen.

"It's got no date marks or reference numbers for a start," Hekla says, turning it over so we can see for ourselves. "And the shape and style of the canister is all wrong. These were only used in the very early days of capture technology. But they were totally unreliable and became easily corrupted over time, so chunks of the capture could go missing," she explains, with the kind of affection that most people reserve for a favourite dog, and she strokes the canister lovingly. "The Institute eventually switched to more stable technology and these became relics. Legend has it that a whole store of these blank captures sat unused for more than a century, and that some of them went missing when a disgruntled tech-head got fired from the sublevels. He probably sold them on the black market and they've been popping up at random ever since. Even I could get hold of one if I paid the right people enough money."

She reaches across the floor and grabs her laptop, quickly bringing up a whole page of pictures showing illegal dark captures that have allegedly been found over the years. They look exactly like the one from Millie's box. Then Hekla turns her attention to the other half of the puzzle my sister has left behind.

"And this is a really ancient capture machine." She gently places the machine next to the canister, searches the outside for a reference number, and taps it into her laptop. "This is the same one that was stolen from the Institute just over six years ago," she says, pointing out the numbers which match those quoted in a dozen different articles reporting the theft. "Millie must have taken it so she could make this dark capture."

"I bet this is the idea that Kit was trying to talk her out of," I say, picking up the capture machine. It's surprisingly light and I can balance it easily in the palm of my hand. "If she was planning to make a dark capture, she must have stolen this machine from the Institute first." I have a sudden absurd image of my sister sneaking into the large open concourse, in the dead of night, with a crowbar and a black balaclava covering her silvery Hummingtree hair. But nothing about this is remotely funny.

"Well, we're dead meat if anyone ever finds out we've got this," Hekla says. "If we'd broken into Cassian Cromwell's home and stolen his personal collection of diamond-studded toothpicks it would have been less serious than this. Millie must have been out of her mind."

Or maybe she was just desperate. The trail that has led to this dark capture has been planned with precision. The captures delivered on the sixth anniversary of her death, so carefully chosen, the LondonCall message sending me to the Wall of the Dead. Whatever she's trying to tell me, she went to a lot of trouble, and law-breaking, to do it.

"So let's take this capture back to the booth at Kaida's flat and find out what it is," Wren says, already rising from the floor, keen to know exactly what message Millie has left behind. But Hekla grabs a fistful of his sweatshirt and pulls him forcefully back to the floor again.

"Not so fast, McKenzie boy, just sit down and listen," she says. "This capture won't play in any of the modern booths at the college, and all the private booths were converted years ago, including the one at Kaida's place."

Wren frowns. "How do you know so much about capture booths?"

"Some people like to run around a muddy field playing idiotic sports, others like to stuff their faces with popcorn in a movie theatre. I like to know everything it's possible to know about capture technology."

"So you're basically a geek," Wren says, with a cautious look of admiration.

Hekla's eyes flicker, but she stores this new comment away, for future reference, along with the earlier one about the mess in her room. I'll definitely have to warn Wren now because he's crossed a big ugly red line. Nobody calls Hekla a geek and lives to tell the tale.

"So is there anywhere we can actually play this capture?" I ask, trying to get the conversation back on track.

"Well, we could walk into Scrim's office, when she gets back from New York, and ask politely if we can use her own personal booth," Hekla suggests, with an overly bright, sarcastic tone to her voice. "If you're such good buddies with her, she's bound to say yes."

"Or?" I ask, hoping there's another option, because Scrim's allegiance to my family definitely doesn't stretch to the viewing of dark captures.

"Or the only other place I know that still plays this older style of capture is down in the sublevels, booths number nine, ten, eleven and twelve."

Hekla shakes her head and picks up the canister again as if it's still a puzzle to be solved. But to me, the solution seems ludicrously simple.

132

"So all we need to do is get into the sublevels," I say.

Hekla frowns deeply. "But we can't just break into the place like a gang of thieves."

"Why not?" I say, considering the problem rationally. "I'm already guilty of doing exactly that, according to my faked capture, so I might just as well have the satisfaction of actually committing the crime."

"But what about the security captures?" The question's directed at me but Hekla looks slyly at Wren to see which side of this argument he's taking. "We'll get caught before we get anywhere near the sublevel booths."

"I bet nobody bothers checking the security captures in the middle of the night," I say, hoping it's actually true.

"And we can use our volunteer security passes to get through the doors without anyone knowing." Wren fishes the passes out of his pocket and dangles them by their neck chain. Neither of us goes anywhere without them as they also allow us access back into the living quarters.

Hekla glares at him. "But there's no guarantee the capture will even be usable. The contents could have been corrupted; we could be risking our necks for a completely blank capture."

"I think it's a risk worth taking," Wren says quietly.

I nod in agreement. "And we have to do it tonight."

"Tonight?" Hekla's eyes bulge and she fidgets like a rabbit. "Can't we just think about this ridiculous idea for a month or two first? What's the big rush?"

"Tobias Troy could come calling again first thing tomorrow morning," I explain calmly. "And this time, he's probably going to send me and Wren over Niagara Falls in a barrel. This could literally be our only chance to find out what's on that capture."

We spend the next two hours arguing with Hekla about the sanity of the whole scheme, trying to convince her that breaking into the sublevels is our only option. But all three of us know that after tonight, there will be no going back, no innocence left to plead, no alternatives to the detention centre offered, our guilt will be undeniable. Unless we can prove that captures can be faked. One way or another, this will change everything.

Hekla finally agrees to the plan, even she can't think of an alternative, and then time begins to drag at an unbearably slow pace. We can't even attempt to carry out our crazy plan until everyone at the Institute is tucked up in bed, which means we have almost twelve hours to kill first. Hekla spends most of it on her laptop, forehead creased, fingers twitchy, or cradling the ancient capture machine in her hands, gazing inside, trying to figure out how it works, to unravel one of the greatest secrets of our time. Wren sits in a chair reading tech magazines, but he only turns a page every hour or so, his eyes staring blankly into the distance, so I know he's not really taking any of it in. I sit on the floor, toes digging into the carpet, running through everything Millie has left for me to find, trying to figure out what the capture might reveal. Did she discover that Troy has been faking captures? Will this dark capture prove his guilt beyond any doubt? Or is there something else? Something she couldn't tell me any other way? Something lurking unseen in the shadows of this tangled mess that all three of us are now caught up in?

Halfway through the evening I return from washing my face in the bathroom, and it's obvious, from the tense atmosphere surrounding Hekla and Wren like a blue, flammable haze, that they've been getting to know each other in my absence. And that Hekla has been putting Wren through the usual inquisition she applies to everyone I have contact with. But it's impossible to be angry with her. The fact that she tries to protect me so fiercely is one of the things I love about her most, especially now.

We leave Hekla's flat at ten o'clock that evening with Millie's box and make our way back to the Institute. No one is in the mood for conversation and we ride the gondola in silence, travelling high above the city lights that seem to burn with an extra intensity, as if the whole of London is somehow aware of our intentions. But I can't decide if the lights are a good omen, or a prophecy of our imminent doom, and I eventually close my eyes instead. It's just easier not to look.

At this time of night the Institute is practically empty. We enter the cafeteria from the rooftop garden, making our way carefully down to the Long Walk, seeing no more than a handful of people along the way. Hekla and Wren keep watch while I use my ID to swipe through the first door that leads down into the sublevels. No alarms sound, no security guards appear, all is silent, still and deserted.

By the time we reach the second door at the bottom of the stairs, I'm experiencing an unnerving sense of déjà vu, as if I really have done this before, and it's like I'm back in my very first solo capture again. I'm immensely grateful that this time, I'm not alone. I open the second door without difficulty and we finally enter the sublevels.

"This is creepy," Hekla whispers, staring down the dark corridor ahead of us. "You could die in this place and no one would find you for weeks. It's more like a tomb than anything under The Lid."

I shiver, wishing everyone would stop talking about tombs as we make our way through the final door that stands between us and the sublevel booths. Number nine is silent and empty. We cross the chilly changing room inside, which somehow seems much larger and more intimidating because we're not supposed to be here. And I'm glad I haven't eaten anything for several hours. My insides are now squirming with a worm farm of nerves.

We head straight for the air locked door, but before I can even think about loading the capture Hekla snatches it out of my hand.

"We need to load this and stream it live at the same time, so that everyone can see the truth for themselves," she says. In the silent hours we've all spent together she's been busy forming her own plans. "It's the only way we can convince Cassian Cromwell that captures can be faked." Wren studies her again with wary admiration. Hekla carries on explaining, oblivious. "I just need to hack into this terminal and then I can control it remotely from anywhere," she says, taking a long cable from her coat pocket. She attaches it to the booth terminal at one end and her laptop at the other, and then her fingers are flying across her keyboard like she's playing a complicated concerto on a piano. "Whatever happens in that booth will be seen by anyone who clicks onto my feed. I'll send out an alert to a thousand tech-heads, wake them up, and tell them to pass it on, but I'll block anyone from the Institute so they can't see what's going on. With any luck, we'll be up to fifty thousand viewers in less than five minutes. If I say something about you, Wren and a dark capture this will go beyond viral, I mean we're talking total digital pandemic."

She loads the capture a moment later when she's ready, the screen above the door tells us that it's set in observation mode but gives no other details.

"Are you sure this is a good idea?" Wren says, zipping up his coat as Hekla concentrates on setting up a live feed. "Are you certain you want everyone else to see this with us?"

I'm not certain about anything, but it feels like the right thing to do so I nod. "We're not the only people who deserve to know the truth."

"Plus this is the only way to keep all three of us out of a mouldy jail cell," Hekla says, looking up sharply from her laptop. "I think I've just triggered a silent alarm. No captures are scheduled for this booth until tomorrow lunchtime, and I've just alerted the system to the fact that we're using number nine without permission."

"We'd better hurry before someone comes down to investigate," Wren says, glancing automatically over his shoulder. But it's already too late. All three of us hear the sudden sound of a heavy door closing. It's distant, but the only reason we can hear it at all is because someone has now entered the sublevels, and is on their way down to find out what, or who, has triggered the silent alarm.

"As soon as you've got a live feed up and running, get out of the sublevels, go back to my flat and wait for us there," I tell Hekla, slipping my keys into her pocket, hoping that for once in her life she'll actually listen and do as I ask.

"Okay, but I'm not facing the fallout from this alone, so you two had better come out of there alive." The fact that she's included Wren in this warning means he must have stood up well to her earlier inquisition.

I hug her quickly, hoping that this ends with all three of us still on the right side of the living. Wren pulls on his gloves and tucks his springy hair under his hat. And as soon as Hekla's ready, I open the door and enter the booth before second thoughts and doubts can burrow under my skin, and transform me into Yellabell, the coward.

15
Rift

I stand with muscles tensed, ready to run if we're about to be dumped somewhere life-threatening. It's difficult to control my nerves, and the tremor in my left hand threatens to unravel me inwards, like a loose thread. It takes ages for our new surroundings to fully emerge around us; everything seems blurry, like a camera searching for a point of focus on a foggy day. And then I'm almost shocked at how ordinary everything looks. We're standing in a small, dimly lit room that could only be described as shabby. The furniture is well used and unloved, like it's been rescued from a partial incineration. The bed is unmade, the thick curtains drawn even though it's daylight outside. The floor is strewn with discarded clothes and books that I suddenly recognise, things that are so familiar to me I know them almost as well as my own name.

"This stuff belongs to Millie," I tell Wren quietly, feeling my breath quicken. But I don't know the room. It definitely isn't part of the Institute or the college, and I don't understand how some of Millie's possessions, things she's always loved, like her favourite copy of *The Velveteen Rabbit* with its faded yellow cover, could have ended up here.

The person who enters the room from behind us a few seconds later is Kit McKenzie. It's the first time I've seen him without a hood covering his face. His resemblance to Wren is striking. Kit's hair is a shade lighter, he's slightly leaner and taller, but everything else about him is a straight copy, like I'm looking at another version of Wren and I feel an instant warmth towards him. If he was anything like Wren, in any small way, he would have been a great and loyal friend to have. Wren stares at his brother with such an acute mixture of sadness and elation that I look away, and try to let him have a moment of privacy, or as much privacy as he can get with potentially thousands of people already watching our live stream.

Kit crosses the room and knocks on another door. "Millie? Everything's set up the way you wanted it. Are you ready?"

There's a muffled reply and a few seconds later, my sister appears. She walks straight past me, just a few inches away, and even though I've already seen her in three different captures, just days ago, it still gives me a sad kind of thrill to be in her presence again.

The bruises on her skin have faded, she looks fuller in the face than the last time I saw her. She grabs Kit's hand and drags him into the middle of the room like they're about to deliver a scene from a play. She's so close I could reach out and touch her other hand, but she wouldn't feel it, and now is not the time to play at happy family reunions. We have just minutes, maybe less, before the person who's already entered the sublevels shuts this capture down. I shuffle my feet anxiously, willing Millie to speak before her message is lost forever.

"Hey Little Dragon," Millie says with a familiar grin. Both me and Wren automatically shift our positions until we're standing directly in front of Millie and Kit, like we're having a two way conversation. "Congratulations on finding your way to this capture. Sorry about all the cloak and dagger stuff, but we couldn't risk anyone else finding it, and I couldn't tell you everything you need to know on LondonCall."

"You couldn't have put all of this in a nice long letter, instead of a highly illegal dark capture?" Kit asks, but there's a smile on his lips and Millie gently cuffs his ear before turning to face us again.

"You're watching this capture because something bad has happened to us."

The way she says it, so flippantly, so carelessly, almost makes me angry. After everything we've been through, she's going to make a joke out of her own death? But Millie pauses and the humour slowly fades from her face. Whatever she wants to say, it isn't easy, she's struggling to find the right words, and I realise that humour is just a defence.

Kit takes her hand and squeezes it when the silence begins to lengthen. "Just tell your sister the truth," he says gently. "She'll understand; she'll believe you."

Millie nods, taking a shallow breath. I've never seen her look this nervous about anything before.

"Someone at the Institute has been faking captures to recruit volunteers." She says it so plainly that nobody can misunderstand her meaning. "That's how me and Kit both ended up on the programme. Someone has also been taking money from Brimstone Mining and Logging

Corporation, and sending those volunteers into volcanoes and rainforests, to look for sulphur deposits and hardwood trees. And if anyone threatens to tell Cassian Cromwell the truth..." She turns towards the bed, picks up a newspaper and holds it up so we can see the front page in detail. "This is what happens to them."

The picture on the front page clearly shows a massive volcano, mid-eruption, the skies around it are filled with fury, with dense clouds of fire, rock and suffocating pumice. I remember the story with perfect clarity. The eruption made headlines around the world because of the mistaken belief that the volcano was extinct, and that monitoring it for any activity was unnecessary. It was totally unexpected, an out of the blue event and I read every article, watched every news cycle, clinging to the details as if they could somehow save me from—

The muscles in my chest suddenly tighten. I know exactly what Millie's about to say. I'm tied to the rail tracks and I can feel it speeding towards me like a runaway freight train. The date at the top of the front page, almost six years ago now, confirms the impossible truth.

Millie is holding a newspaper that was printed three weeks after she and Kit supposedly died. The capture that showed them both being killed in a rockslide was a fake. Which means my sister and Wren's brother are still alive.

Wren frowns at the paper, unaware of the significance of the picture, impatient to hear what Millie has to say. I'm beyond desperate to explain, but I'm also too afraid to move. All of this will disappear, like dandelion clocks scattered on a summer breeze, if I allow myself a single blink of an eye, if I breathe too quickly or even think the wrong thoughts, all of this will dissolve away to nothing, like some kind of tragic hallucination.

I stand so rigidly that my muscles begin to cramp. Millie folds the paper with an anxious smile. She's about to deliver her shocking revelation to us, and to everyone who is now watching this live capture stream, when it happens. The room we're standing in begins to shudder, there's a familiar flickering in the air; Millie and Kit fade away to nothing and I'm staring at the bare bedrock walls of booth number nine instead. I feel the wrench in my gut like I've just lost my sister all over again.

"The capture must be corrupted," Wren says, agitated and angry at the disruption. "Hekla warned us this could happen. Or maybe someone at the Institute has already pulled the capture, before Mille can drop any more bombshells."

Bombshells have got nothing on the news that Millie was just about to deliver. But if Millie can't tell the world that she and Kit are still alive, that the capture showing how they died in a rockslide was totally faked, then it's up to me. And I've got to do it quickly, before our live stream is severed. I tug urgently on Wren's coat sleeve and he turns, but there's another sudden change, another unexpected shift in location. The ground beneath our feet moves and stirs with such force, that it throws us both off balance. It now feels bitterly cold and a blast of super-chilled air whittles me down to the bone like a carving knife. The light levels dim but there's an unearthly, silvery sheen that casts everything around us into muted shadows. When the confusion clears, we're standing on the vast white expanse of a glacier, a solid ribbon of ice that fills the floor of a wide, steep valley. A full moon has risen, emitting its eerie glow over the dark landscape. The glacier is immense, powerful, bleakly magnificent. My head is spinning at such a rapid change and it's so disorientating that I almost throw up. Wren staggers sideways, slipping on the ice as we both try to get our bearings in this barren land.

This has got nothing to do with Millie, Kit or Hekla; someone has loaded a new capture. And I know we're in big trouble.

"Tobias Troy," Wren says, his skin already turning a mottled blue with cold. "He knows we're in here. He's trying to finish what he started with the truck ride."

If Troy is truly unaware that everything that happens inside this booth is being streamed live, that his second attempt to kill us is being witnessed by the world, if he thinks he can get away with it because Aldora Scrim is still in New York...then he chose this capture for a good reason. Danger is already heading towards us, whether we can see it or not. And we're far too vulnerable and exposed standing out here in the middle of the ice.

"We should head for the side of the valley, climb up onto the rocks," I say, zipping up my coat, pulling on my hat and gloves, wishing I'd worn more layers. I have to force all thoughts of Millie and Kit aside, because nothing is more important than getting off this glacier, before it breaks apart and swallows us whole. I'll tell Wren about his living, breathing, back-from-the-dead brother when we're safe.

But reaching solid ground won't be easy. I know, from studying the work of LoveNature Eternal, that these huge bodies of unpredictable ice are perforated with hidden caves, and powder-thin snow bridges, that could collapse without warning under our weight. But the person who took this capture must have made it to this spot somehow, I realise.

I scan the horizon. The only sign that any other human has ever walked on this glacier sits on top of a small rise in the ice: a single ice axe, and a collection of crampons for walking on slippery surfaces, probably worn by the captologist.

"Over there!" I pull Wren towards the equipment and it's a struggle just to keep ourselves upright on the treacherous glacier. Wren grabs the axe and we both secure the crampons over our boots. But I can't shake the feeling that this ancient body of ice is a malevolent creature, and I'm already half expecting to feel it shudder and stir beneath me, when the first tremor hits.

"What's happening?" Wren asks, trying to keep his balance as the ground rumbles beneath us, the monster already waking.

"The glacier's unstable, it's moving the whole time. We have to get onto solid ground."

But from our slightly raised vantage point, it's clear that the glacier is riddled with dangerous crevasses and rifts, running like the tributaries of a river, they cut off every route to safe ground. It's Wren who spots the ladder. It's been placed across a deep cleft fifty feet away, forming a makeshift bridge, like the captologist who brought it here was playing snakes and ladders with their life. When we reach it, it's obvious that the ladder is a death trap.

"The rungs are rotten, it won't take our weight," I say, inspecting the flimsy looking structure.

Wren balances his whole weight on the first rung, testing it out to see if it can take the strain. It sinks a little deeper into the ice, but holds firm. We have no choice but to cross it.

"You go first," he says. "I can kneel on the ladder at this end and hold it steady."

I'm shaking violently before I even approach the first rung. As soon as my left foot touches the ladder I feel it quiver beneath me. This is a death walk, a thousand times more terrifying than the metal walkway outside the rooftop booth at home, but that's exactly what it reminds me of.

"Keep looking straight ahead, Kaida," Wren says calmly. "Take it one step at a time."

I place my right foot in front of my left, fully aware that I've now left solid ground, that I'm suspended above a deep crevasse. I slide my feet slowly, and by the time I'm halfway across, I'm trembling almost as much as the ladder, which wobbles precariously under the burden of my footfalls. I can sense the sinister void beneath me, waiting for one accidental slip, one badly placed boot that will send me tumbling. For a moment, my knees lock solid and I can't move an inch further.

"You're almost there, Kaida." Wren's voice is deliberately calm and soothing, and somehow it frees me up to move again.

I edge slowly forwards, with brittle limbs and short gasping breaths. But my crampon slips across the rung beneath me and I fall heavily onto my left knee, my hands groping for the next rung to stop me from plunging any further. The ladder jolts and bends before it settles again, and I cling to it, limpet-like, too petrified to breathe, move or open my eyes.

"Are you okay?" Wren's voice sounds distant, drowned out by the terror pounding in my ears. I manage to nod my head but even such a small movement causes the ladder to shift again, creaking and groaning in protest. I'll have to cross the rest of the death walk on my hands and knees, my legs are way too traumatised to hold me upright.

I focus on the rocks in the distance, forbidding myself to glance down and stare into the abyss, but my whole body shakes. When I finally make it, I sprawl out onto the ice, facing the stars above, thanking every god that may or may not exist, for my safe passage.

By the time I haul myself up into a seated position, Wren already has one foot on the ladder, testing the springiness and his balance. Before I have a chance to worry, he glides across the rungs in an easy, fluid string of steps, making my pathetic efforts look like a huge fuss about nothing. Anyone else would gloat, but Wren just helps me up to my feet and wraps his arms around me.

"Try not to trip again," he says, with a gentle lean of his head against mine. "I almost left a yellow puddle on the ice."

He takes my hand and I'm grateful for the support. My legs are still dangerously unsteady, my heart still hammering hard. But as he leads us closer to the side of the valley I stop, digging my crampons into the surface of the glacier.

"What?" Wren asks, his grip tightening. He tries to pull me onwards, but I stand my ground.

"Wren, the capture with Kit and Millie, I know what she was about to say," I tell him, watching a flicker of surprise cross his face.

"Can't this wait until we reach the rocks?" he asks, glancing over his shoulder to safer ground, now tantalizingly close.

But I shake my head. "I need to tell you now," I say, knowing that if the ice monster wins, he'll never hear the truth about this brother. So I tell him as quickly as I can, explaining about the newspaper that Millie showed us, how I am sure of the date, and the fact that the eruption happened after his brother was supposed to be dead.

There's a tiny pause, a moment of pure, moonlit silence, then Wren buries his face in his hands, his whole body suddenly shaking. When he finally looks up again, his face is a mess, a blotchy-skinned canvas smeared with tears, his eyebrows pointing in a dozen different directions. And it's the sight of his eyebrows that finally tips me over the edge. I've got no control over the tremors that start from the inside and work their way out of my body in spasms. All these years without Millie, only alive in my memories, always hovering just out of reach, and now I understand why I could never fully let her go. Some part of me knew that she wasn't really gone, that someday I would get her back...but only if we can make it out of this capture alive.

"Are you certain?" Wren eventually asks, his voice raw and broken.

I manage a single nod before the spasms start again. The shaking inside my body is suddenly mirrored by another ice tremor, this one more violent and prolonged than the others; the tension in the ice monster is building. We have to get off the glacier.

Wren is already running towards the rocky side of the valley, glancing over his shoulder every few seconds to make sure I'm still following close behind. It's hard going in my boots, even with the crampons, and my feet slide out from underneath me every few steps, my arms wind-milling wildly just to keep me upright.

Wren leaps over a small foot-wide fissure in the ice, and this time, I have no choice but to jump without looking, no hesitations, no time for panic or palpitations. We're almost three quarters of the way across the glacier when Wren stops abruptly, standing stiff and straight.

"What is it?" I slide to a halt beside him, scanning the horizon, searching for the head of the ice creature that we've woken. We both hear a long grumbling moan and I feel the tremor through the soles of my boots, then the ground begins to give way. "We're standing on a snow bridge!" I yell above the gathering noise. "It can't take our weight; we've got to move, now!"

We instinctively run away from the sound that seems to follow us, travelling straight through skin and blood. There's a loud crack, a sharp, snapping, gunshot of a sound that bounces off the flanks of the valley walls, and echoes around us, repeating and rolling like thunder. The rocks are now so close I can almost reach out and touch them, but it's already too late. The ground disintegrates beneath us and I'm falling into a crevasse, a weightless tumble that instantly makes me nauseous, and it feels like we're back inside the truck again, out of control, tumbling into oblivion.

16
Lost

I smash into a solid shelf of ice, landing heavily on my ribs. The left side of my body crumples under the force and knocks the breath out of me. I curl up into a tight ball trying to protect my head from the lethal, jagged slabs of ice that plunge and shatter all around me with a cataclysmic sound, like the sky has been unfastened from its celestial bolts and allowed to fall. And then a heavy silence settles.

I roll carefully onto my back, feeling numb with the shock of the fall. I can see a hole, twenty feet above me where the snow bridge has given way. The ice shelf that broke my fall is wide and I can stretch both arms out from my sides without feeling any edge. But there's no sign of Wren.

"Wren?" I try to call his name but there's not enough breath left in my body for anything more than a whisper. I clamber onto my knees, ignoring the pain in my ribs, and stare over the edge of the shelf at the lumpy walls of ice below, blue and undulating, like the stomach lining of a whale. The chasm is so deep I can't even see the bottom.

"Wren?" My voice is louder this time and panic-filled, it echoes around me causing another small slide of ice from above.

But I lean over the edge hoping Wren might have found his own shelf further down. I only notice the ice axe when it swings into a shaft of moonlight, which reflects off the metal blade. It's dug into the ice just five feet beneath me. Wren is gripping onto the handle with both hands and it's clear that he won't be able to hold his own weight for much longer, as he sways above the abyss.

"Kaida, help me!" His voice is more fearful than I've ever heard it before.

I rip off my coat, lean over as far as I dare, digging the spikes of my crampons into the ice, then I dangle a sleeve down towards him. "Wrap this around your arm!" I say, doing the only thing I can think of to help. He tries to grasp the coat, legs flailing wildly over the deep hole and he somehow manages to loop the material around his forearm several times. I shuffle back from the edge and then brace myself against the wall of the crevasse, feet wedged by the heels in front of me. "Use the axe to pull yourself up!"

I'm now Wren's only lifeline and anchor. I can barely hold his weight and I'm praying to the gods of fabric that the coat won't rip or tear along the seams. I clench my jaw and hold on tight, listening as Wren tries to work the axe free from the ice. He finally manages to tug the blade out and then digs it in again, hauling himself upwards, towards the lip of the shelf, but his breathing is now erratic and raw.

"I can't feel my fingers!" he says, and I can hear the pain and terror in his voice.

"You've got to hold on!" I tell him sternly. "You've got to get out of this capture so you can watch Kit's dinosaur impressions again. He owes you a really good one after all these years!"

Everything goes eerily quiet and still. There's an abrupt shifting of weight. The coat pulls tight, yanking on my arms and I have to fight to stop myself from being dragged forward. Then it suddenly goes limp.

"Wren!" I yell, frantically removing my feet from their dug-in position and scrambling over to the edge of the shelf. I can still see the axe, just two feet beneath me now, but Wren is no longer attached to it. "Wren!"

The only answering call is my own voice, echoing around the chasm like the cry of a ghost, and I know I've lost him.

I try to carry on breathing but nothing makes it down to my lungs, and I start choking on my own tears instead. More than anything else I feel numb, like the part of my brain that registers grief and shock and death has temporarily shut down, and the tears quickly dry up too.

I sit for a long time, hugging my knees, wondering why nobody has pulled the capture, why nobody has stopped Tobias Troy. But it's already too late; the damage can never be undone. Nobody can bring someone back from the dead, not even with all the genius-grade technology at the Cromwell Institute. I'll never see Wren again. The best friend I've ever had, besides Hekla, and now he's gone.

I finally start to shiver with cold and I know I have to make a choice. There's a part of me that wants to stay here until the dawn breaks, or hypothermia takes my body, so I can be with Wren to the bitter end. But I also know that I can't give up now, that for Wren's sake, I've got to see this through to the end of my own story. I stare up at the hole in the ice, twenty feet above. There's no sign of a rescue party, so I'll have to rescue myself from this slippery grave.

At the far edge of the hole, furthest away from me, there's a narrowing where the ice forms a sort of chimney. If I can reach it, I might be able to climb up using the axe.

I shuffle along and peer over the side of my shelf. There's another ledge just four feet below me, it hugs the side of the crevasse and runs parallel to the hole above. I can follow it all the way to the chimney, but I'll have to jump down to it first. Fear of the abyss swells inside my chest and almost stops me breathing again. My head spins and I have to lean against the wall until the dizzy spell passes.

I pull on my coat and manage to work the axe free from the ice without dropping it, and then I have to summon up the courage to jump. I think about Wren, with his easy grace and strength, then I back up as far as I dare and take a running leap. My feet land heavily and for a moment I'm terrified that the ledge is about to give way beneath me, but the ice holds firm. I move carefully along the narrow shelf until I'm directly beneath the spot where the ice narrows. I brace my body against the sides of the chimney, using the axe to anchor me in place while I dig my crampons in and shift my weight, inching upwards, awkwardly, slowly.

The climb takes forever. It's harder than anything I've done in any other capture; I'd gladly take three muddy rainforest rivers over this muscle-cramping torture. By the time the blade of my axe finally breaks free of the crevasse, and sinks into solid ice above ground, the sun is already starting to rise. With one last effort, I drag myself out of the rift, breathing heavily, too exhausted and numb to feel any relief.

I roll onto my back, sprawled across the ice, staring at the vast expanse above, feeling the glacier move beneath my body. A crack runs right beside me, deep enough to form another crevasse under the right pressure. I don't want to be here when it happens, so I clamber to my feet, hoping to reach the valley rocks without another tumble into the icy underworld. And that's when I see three figures heading towards me.

Aldora Scrim, flanked on both sides by a college security guard, wearing a long emerald-green cape she glides like a snow queen, imperious and all powerful. For a moment, I don't trust my own senses and I wonder if she's nothing more than a hallucination, or some kind of peculiar glacier mirage, brought on by trauma and bone-deep tiredness. But the mirage continues to head straight towards me. I catch a faint trace of heavy vanilla-scented perfume on the breeze, and I know Scrim must be real. I'm so relieved that someone has finally come to help, and I'm about to close the gap between us, to tell her everything about Wren, Millie, Kit and Tobias Troy, when a nagging doubt stops me. And I can't ignore it, no matter how much I'd like to.

Why has Scrim entered the capture at all? Why hasn't she just yanked me out of the booth and hurried me over to the hospital, or into her office, where we could sort this whole tragedy out in private?

"I must confess myself very disappointed in you, Kaida," she says by way of a greeting that sounds a lot frostier than usual. The guards stand silently beside her, their skin protected from the bitter cold by balaclavas and deep hoods. "When you used your pass to break into the sublevels you triggered an automatic alarm in the security wing. And then you loaded a dark capture. Yet more crimes to add to the growing list you appear to be guilty of committing."

"But, haven't you come to help me?" I ask uncertain, staring at Scrim, wondering why she hasn't mentioned anything about the capture we're standing in, why she hasn't asked about my sister.

And the truth hits me so hard I almost puke at her feet. It's because she already knows everything.

"This has gone far enough, Kaida," Scrim says as if we're still connected by some false family loyalty. But the veneer of kindness has been scrubbed from her face, leaving nothing behind but the true ugliness of her soul. "You've crossed too many lines and now it has to stop."

She pauses, waiting for me to explain myself, but I hold my silence. Hekla has done her job well, keeping this live stream away from anyone at the Institute. Scrim has no idea that our conversation is being witnessed by thousands of people, she truly believes we're alone. But I'm hoping that everyone who is now watching has just realised what Scrim has done, that they can see who she really is, now that her facade has fallen away.

"Where's Millie, what have you done with her?" I ask, trying to get my facts straight, which ones are real, which ones have been faked.

Aldora Scrim is behind every lie I've heard. She pretended to believe my story when I first got shown into her office, vowing to discover the truth, offering me an alternative to the detention centre, knowing all along that volunteering would ultimately end in my death, a death that she herself would arrange when I stopped being useful. Me, Hekla and Wren have been looking for answers in all the wrong places.

"You faked the capture where my sister and Wren's brother died, and now Wren's dead for real." I sway dizzily as I say the words out loud, but I no longer feel numb. "You've been taking money from Brimstone, so they can look for sulphur deposits in volcanoes and hardwood trees in rainforests," I say, determined to lay everything bare before our audience. "You've been forcing volunteers to do your dirty work, so they'll keep their mouths shut and their suspicions to themselves."

The smug, satisfied look on Scrim's face is better than any confession, she's proud of her achievements. I feel like I'm seeing her true face for the first time in my life.

"I had no choice but to have Millie volunteered. She overheard me talking to Troy about Brimstone on my phone, at the flat, the day of her sixteenth birthday," Scrim explains calmly. "Millie waited several weeks to confront me in person, and she was very indignant about it. But even as a volunteer she continued to threaten me with exposure. I'd already arranged it with Troy that Millie and the McKenzie boy would both die in a dangerous capture, and then the stupid little minx ran away."

The venom in her words is almost more shocking than the crimes she has committed and I take an unconscious step away from her.

"The only way I could be sure of her silence then was to threaten your safety, Kaida. And so my hand was forced again," Scrim says, trying to make it sound like this is somehow my fault, Millie's fault. "You have proven just as troublesome as your sister. But I see I've made the right decision about your future, this capture was the perfect one to choose. It's far tidier to end it here."

"You're going to kill me so I can't tell anyone what you've done?" I ask, making things as plain as possible, so there can be no misunderstanding.

"You must admit it's a neat little ending to your tragic tale," Scrim says. "And it will make sensational headlines, when the world hears that you've followed the same sad fate as your sister, that Wren McKenzie abandoned you to your death, a cowardly action to rival that of his brother's. All I have to do is fake a capture that tells the world exactly what I want it to believe, and no one will question a thing. You will become an instant legend, and Cassian Cromwell will be none the wiser about what's really happening at his Institute."

I say nothing, letting her reveal the shocking depths of her deceit and greed, even though her words fill me with wild-cat rage. I've trusted her for so many years, believed in her kindness and benevolence, and in return she's ripped my family apart for money.

She pulls her cloak around her for warmth, with the same air of arrogant satisfaction. Then she turns to the security guards. "Push her over the edge and let's get out of here. We'll send a team in to scrape up the mess when the capture ends."

I lunge for the axe before the guards can make the first move, tugging it out of the ice and hurling it clumsily in Scrim's direction. Then I run, dodging through the chaos of grabbing and shouting that follows. Scrim wails at her guards like a banshee. One of them gets a good hold on my arm. I dig my nails into his skin and yank myself free. But the other guard rams into me with his shoulder, knocking me off my feet, and I hit the ground painfully, face first. He takes my ankle then and begins to drag me back towards the crevasse. I try to gouge my fingers into the ice, attempting to slow our progress, to hold my ground, but the frozen surface is too hard and I'm not strong enough to break it. The guard starts to swing my body round to the right in a wide circle as we near the chasm, he's clearly intending to fling me into the hole like a carcass, and I'm inches away from being dead meat. The chances of landing on another ice shelf are too slim to count. For the third time in as many days I'm hurtling towards the edge of death, and something in me finally snaps. I can't take another brush with the Grim Reaper.

I twist round suddenly, flipping over, using the guard's grip on my ankle as leverage, until I'm lying on my back. Then I kick out with my free foot and slice his hand open with my crampons. The man lets go of my ankle with a volley of curses and rips off his balaclava, so he can inspect the damage to his hand.

Tobias Troy. Come to help Scrim, just like he's been doing for years. And now he's going to ensure that every trace of my existence is destroyed. I have to act before the deadly duo fake my death as well as my life.

The ice axe is now just a few strides away and I'm closer to it than anyone else. I scramble to my feet, Scrim realises what I'm intending to do but I'm too quick for her. I grab the axe for a second time and throw it hard, aiming at her body, hoping to stop her in her tracks and give someone the opportunity to end this capture before it ends me. She dodges clumsily to the left, cursing all the days that me and the rest of my family were born, but she's unharmed. Troy tackles me to the ground before I can inflict any real damage, and my head hits the slippery ice hard. Pain fans out from one side of my skull to the other and it feels like a cracked egg. I thrash my legs, trying to score another strike with my crampons, but I get a knee in my back for my efforts and I'm pinned to the ground, under a solid mountain of muscle and hatred.

"Stop struggling, there's nowhere left to run," Troy hisses in my ear, and I can smell the sharp tang of his blood as it drips onto the ice beside me. I can also feel how badly he wants to hurt me, how much he longs to crush my bones into the ice. Scrim's presence is the only thing that restrains him. But even she won't be able to hold him back for long.

"It would have been so much easier just to take your punishment, Kaida." Scrim's voice is velvet soft, a cat's purr; it drifts in and out of focus as my head throbs. She stalks around me, a wolf deciding which part of its prey to devour first. Then she crouches down, brushing a stray strand of silvery hair out of my eyes. "But you always were the one with a fire in your belly, Little Dragon."

She nods at Troy who still has his knee in my back, and then she stands and turns away. And that's when the creature crawls out of the crevasse. With a skin like shattered diamonds, eyes of summer blue, it rests on its haunches and then explodes at Troy, drawing a long steely talon from the ice. It pushes Troy off balance and I'm suddenly free. I manage to haul myself upright as feet pound across the surface of the glacier sending tremors through the ice. The creature is now wielding an axe and it looks exactly like Wren, I realise, with a jolt of surprise. But I can't think clearly enough to understand what I'm seeing, everything is a troubling haze.

The Wren creature charges at Tobias Troy like a bull with a thorny-prickled foot. I try to focus my eyes but a fuzzy shape blocks my view and takes my arm firmly. Scrim drags me towards the edge of the crevasse clearly intending to finish the job herself, to fling me into the icy blue rift and destroy my family for a second time.

"Time to meet your fate, Kaida," she says coldly.

I struggle against her grip, but she's too strong for me to win this fight.

151

The scent of vanilla is now so odorous that it seems to hang in the air like a noxious gas, and it's the abhorrent smell that finally frees me from my brain fog for long enough to act. I jab my spikes into the ice and deliberately tumble backwards, landing so hard on my tailbone that stars dance before my eyes. Scrim loses her hold on my arm and trips over my feet. She staggers forwards, arms stretched out to brace her body against the fall, but there's now nothing left between her and the wide hole in the ice. She tumbles over the edge leaving a vivid imprint of disbelief and terror behind her. For a moment, it sounds like the crevasse itself is screaming with a terrible, echoing cry that sends shivers through my feet. I hold my breath, imagining I can hear the precise moment her body hits the floor of the chasm. Then all I can hear is my own erratic breathing.

Wren is suddenly at my side, he's got a split lip and a swollen eye but he's mercifully whole and alive. Troy and the other guard are fleeing in the opposite direction, not willing to sacrifice themselves without their leader's protection, Troy's mile-wide streak of coward revealing itself for everyone now watching our live feed to devour and enjoy.

"I couldn't hold onto you and you fell," I say, blinking at the face that swims before me, still a little out of focus. My thoughts feel just as fuzzy, like I'm trying to dredge them up from the depths of a muddy swamp. "I thought you were dead."

"I nearly was," Wren says, sounding exhausted by our ordeal, and he sits on the ice beside me, arms draped over his knees. "When I couldn't hold onto the axe any longer, I fell straight through the top of an ice tunnel. I had to crawl along the inside until I found a way out, and then climb up the side of the crevasse. It's like a maze down there; I thought I'd never find you again."

Wren smiles at me from sheer relief and it's so unbelievably good to see his friendly face. I still can't grasp that he's truly alive, and I keep my fingers crossed that when my head hit the ice, it didn't somehow shatter my slender grip on reality, that I'm not sitting here by myself now, speaking with nothing more than ghosts and memories.

Scrim was right about one thing. Me and Wren will be legends now. We've just delivered the most thrilling end to the biggest drama ever to come out of the Institute. But all I want to do is take my battered body home, to sit at the kitchen table with Millie, Yarena and Hekla, and listen to the safe humming of the fridge.

17
The Faithful

Two months later.

The Long Walk is so peaceful that it could be Christmas. The bank of mirrored lifts, usually so crowded at this time of day, stands quiet and deserted. I push one of the buttons as I walk past, just to hear the familiar *ping* of the bell as the door opens. But I don't feel like stopping, I want to get up to the flat on the fifth floor as quickly as possible. It's the first time I've been allowed home in two months, the first time I've been back to the Institute since everything that happened in booth number nine.

My memories of the days that followed are vague and disorientating, and sometimes, I'm not sure which ones are real, and which ones are caused by the concussion I suffered at the hands of Tobias Troy. But these facts I know for sure.

I spent three days in the hospital, semi-conscious and confused, followed by a longer trip to Northumberland to stay with Grandma and Grandpa Hummingtree, so I'm nowhere near the Institute in the aftermath. Endless news cycles pick over every tiny detail of Aldora Scrim's crimes, how she and Tobias Troy planned the whole scheme together and carried it out with ruthless ambition. Troy is caught and arrested before he can escape London's city limits. His trial is swift and decisive; he will spend the rest of his life in jail for the part he played, for condemning so many volunteers to serious injury or worse. Cassian Cromwell temporarily suspends all capture taking and closes the Institute, until a thorough investigation into everything that's happened has taken place. Until someone has figured out just how many captures might have been faked over the years, and what the consequences might be.

Pictures of Millie and Kit are shown on an everlasting loop, the real cause of their disappearance discussed and dissected in minute detail. The media storm surrounding it all is relentless and overwhelming. And then the questions come.

How could Cassian Cromwell let this happen? How could he not know that captures can be faked, that deals were being made and volunteers used in such dreadful circumstances? How can the Institute ever survive this devastating scandal? What use are captures if they can be faked?

Me and Hekla discuss every question in detail when Grandma Hummingtree finally lets me speak to her on LondonCall. I'm so happy to see her face again that for the first ten minutes, I can't stop grinning. But the topic I want to discuss with her most is the live capture feed she set up from booth number nine.

"After you and Wren disappeared inside, I went straight up to your flat, just like you said," she tells me looking pleased with herself for obeying my orders. "I tried to pull the capture as soon as the glacier appeared," she explains. "But some rogue tech-head had already hijacked my live feed, and I couldn't stop it. Some snivelling little techie geek wanted all the glory, and now nobody even knows it was me who set it up in the first place."

"At least you won't have to give up your hacking habit any time soon," I say, trying to salvage something positive from the situation.

Hekla smiles broadly. "I've already thought of that."

There's another memory, one that is now etched upon my brain more clearly than any extraordinary moment of captured time. The morning after, in the hospital, I wake feeling like I've been trampled by a stampede of wild horses, every hair on my head hurts, ever joint, muscle, bone, fingernail and earlobe is burning with pain. There's a comforting weight on the end of my bed, just like so many times before, a phantom from the past that will disappear the instant I open my eyes. But this time, the weight remains and I see a familiar face staring back at me, eyes blinking in the semi-darkness of the room.

Millie, my big sister. Back from the dead after six long years.

She's older, not exactly the way I remember her, her eyes are a deeper shade of green, her silvery hair is scraped back into a ponytail, lank-looking and grubby. Her features have matured and lost the last traces of childhood, she's a grown woman now. The six years that we've been separated have altered her. But she's still my sister and I feel it in every aching bruise on my body.

"Hey, Little Dragon," she says, so softly it's almost a whisper.

I'm incapable of any answer; my head is a throbbing cave, filled with lightning-strike pain. But my pulse begins to climb. Tears slide down my face and soak into my hair, sticking my eyelashes together so the edges of the room blur.

"I'm not supposed to hug you," she says, pulling a face. "The doctor's given me ten minutes, then she's yanking me out. But I wanted to see you for myself."

I must look pretty beaten up because her features suddenly twist, like she's found a mangy dog in the street, and decided to take it home and nurse it back to health. She holds my hand and squeezes it gently. I'm ridiculously grateful for the pain it causes.

"Me and Kit," she says, slowly, carefully, "Scrim wanted everyone to believe that we hated each other, so she fed the media with stories about us arguing, right from the very moment we met," Millie explains, eager to help me understand. "I'm sorry I couldn't tell you the truth, but Scrim warned that if I didn't keep my silence about being volunteered, about Brimstone, that she'd make sure you never saw your sixteenth birthday. It was safer for you and everyone else to believe the lies."

She grips my hand even harder and this time, I manage a superhuman feat of brain-muscle-coordination, and squeeze back.

"But we both knew we had to leave the Institute, Scrim never had any intention of letting us live. Kit had a trusted friend who lived on a remote farm in North Wales, so we planned our escape," Millie says, leaning in, telling the tale now like it's a storybook adventure that she's trying to convince me is real. "I put in a paper request for the captures that would someday show you what had really happened to me, that would lead you to my message on LondonCall. I stole a capture machine when all the security and alarms had been turned off, when the maintenance staff had unlocked the display case for cleaning. I'd been watching them do it for weeks, so I knew they were careless, and that I could get away with it if I was quick. But on the very morning that we were planning to use it, to make a dark capture and tell you everything about Scrim, on the very morning I sent you that last message on LondonCall, Kit discovered that Troy was going to put us through a crazy training capture, a runaway truck down a mountain path. And we had to leave almost everything behind and run."

I swallow hard, knowing that only luck would have kept Millie and Kit from the same horrible fate that almost killed me and Wren.

"It took us over a week to walk from London to Wales, but five days after we arrived, we saw the faked capture, the one where me and Kit supposedly died. And I knew I had to do more to protect you." She's angry, a flash of the old Millie rising up, animating her features. "So we made the dark capture at the farm and Kit's friend placed it in the Wall of the Dead, in a spot we'd already picked out, the one I told you about on my LondonCall message, just as we'd always intended. I knew it would be years after my so-called death until you found the trail we'd left behind. I had no idea Scrim was planning to have you volunteered too. But I'm so proud of you, Kaida," she says smiling. "And I'm sorry I almost got you killed. We were watching the live feed, and when I saw you and Wren falling into the crevasse..."

We sit in silence for several minutes, both knowing how lucky we've been to survive Aldora Scrim, how her greed almost killed us both. Then the doctor gently taps on the door and it's clearly time for Millie to leave. I'm still struggling to believe that she's real, or that she'll ever come back again if she walks out the door. But I can't hold onto her hand forever.

Millie slides off the bedcovers and picks up my faithful old boots, which I made Yarena leave by the side of my bed, blaming the concussion for my diva-like demands.

"Thanks for looking after my favourite boots, by the way," Millie says, running her hands lovingly over their familiar heels and toes, carefully inspecting the recent battle scars they've accumulated. "But I think these belong to you now, Little Dragon."

Two months after that first unforgettable reunion, I walk slowly up the stairs to the flat. Most of my injuries have healed well, apart from a dull night time ache in my ribs from where I landed on the ice shelf. Millie has gone to stay with Kit in Wales, until the future fate of capture technology has been decided and they can return to a normal life. But we've just spent eight glorious weeks together in Northumberland, our family complete once again, with a whole new batch of memories to share, precious and real, no hiding in the shadows.

Yarena meets me in the hallway before I can reach the front door and she hugs me tightly, all my volunteering crimes forgiven the instant she understood I had no choice. She takes my bag and leads the way into the living area, and I'm so happy to be home that all I want to do is sprawl on the sofa, and watch the sun flickers dance around the room. Measles is rolling on the floor by the windows, and crouching down beside her, stroking the soft fur on her belly, is Wren.

"What are you doing here?" I ask, hurrying over, hugging him so tightly that I hear his spine crack.

"Mum and Dad brought me back to the Institute yesterday," he says, pulling away so he can breathe, but he keeps a firm hold on my arm. "And I figured you might want to see my face in person."

I can tell he's missed me just as much as I've missed him. And that the real reason he's here is because the closeness we've now forged will always draw us together.

It's the first contact we've had since the final capture ended, apart from one brief meeting in the hospital, when he snuck into my room and we compared our cuts and bruises, still three parts delirious from everything that had happened.

After that, Wren's parents took him straight from the hospital to stay with Kit in Wales, where Millie has now gone, no LondonCall messages, no old fashioned letters permitted. The time away has clearly allowed all his visible injuries to heal. The hair on the shaved side of his head is now sprouting at odd angles and it will soon be back to its former, untamed glory. There's so much I want to talk to him about, that only he will ever understand fully, but those conversations will have to wait for another day, for a more private moment. I smile at Wren again, feeling immensely grateful that time is now something we've both got plenty of.

Over the next few weeks I spend most of my days in the flat, or visiting Wren, or hanging out in Mole Valley with Hekla. It's impossible to go anywhere else without being recognised. Me and Wren still feature in many of the news reports, nobody seems to tire of the sensational footage in our last capture, and we are called every version of heroic, brave and courageous under the sun. But that's not how I feel. If my time as a volunteer has shown me anything, it's that I'm definitely not cut out for a life of daredevil danger and uncertainty. Instinct and luck kept me alive. And Wren. Without Wren I would have perished in the rainforest fire. But I also finally have the answer to the question that has haunted me for years.

Despite everything that's happened, despite all the times I nearly died, a captologist is still the only thing I truly want to be. For better or worse, I now know that my love of captures stems from the very heart of me, and that nothing will ever shake that feeling loose, not even volcanoes or glaciers.

Kaida Hummingtree, trainee captologist.

That's a future I can live with.

Coming Soon...

Shadow in the Starlight

*Exclusive extract from a
new book by Annie Hoad*

Chapter 1

There was only one way to reach the tiny town of Oakheaven. And that was to follow the creepy, winding, gloomy road that skirted the edge of an ancient woodland, while trying not to scream your lungs out.

I stared out the car window as we travelled past the endless parade of trees. In the early winter darkness, even the deep gaps between the prehistoric-looking oaks seemed menacing. Everything was too still, too silent somehow. As if the trees were planning something sinister.

I sighed and turned, looking straight through the windscreen. The fact that I thought the trees had plans was the most worrying fact of all. I'd always had an overactive imagination. Sometimes, it was impossible to get it under control.

"Something funny?" Mum asked from the driver's seat, seeing a wry smile cross my face.

I shrugged. "I was just wondering about the wood. What's it called again?"

"Shadow Wood." Mum paused letting the words vibrate around the interior of our car. "Isn't it the most perfect name?"

I shivered. It was an exquisite mix of sinister and threatening.

"And you're positive there aren't any bears, wolves or trolls living in there?" I asked, scanning the dark gaps between the trees for eyes.

"Well, I'm not a hundred percent sure about the trolls." Mum smiled as we finally reached the outskirts of Oakheaven, marked by a sudden thinning of the trees, and a row of thatched cottages peppered with street lamps. "Just wait until you see this place in the daylight. The whole town's like something out of a fairytale."

Fabulous. Just what me and my imagination needed. As we pulled up outside the museum a moment later, it was clear that neither of us was ever going to get any rest in Oakheaven.

"This is it," Mum said as the car stuttered to a halt. "So, what do you think of our new home? Isn't it adorable?"

The museum was a heavy-set Victorian building, red brick, austere, the kind that hunchbacks and vampires preferred above all others. Normally, I loved any building of age; The Natural History Museum, The Tower of London and several Scottish castles were already among my particular favourites. But I'd never lived in any place with its own gargoyles before and the thought was already making me nervous. I searched the night skies for the lightning bolt that must have been desperate to strike the gothic monstrosity before us. But the lightning was picking its moment.

"It's really great, Mum," I said, trying to sound genuine.

"Okay, so I'll admit it's a little on the creepy side, but it's an incredible place, Pru." Mum gave my arm an excited squeeze as she opened the door, and went to retrieve our bags from the boot.

I gathered up my hat and gloves from the foot well and stepped into the icy air outside, staring up at the gothic monstrosity. There were only three things I knew about the museum. It had been built in the 1850s. It was surrounded by ancient woodland, which cut the whole town of Oakheaven off from the rest of civilisation. And Mum had come to rescue it. Like a spectacle-wearing, artefact-protecting, super-curator she was attuned to the distress calls sent out by all sick and ailing museums across the globe. She then swooped in and dragged them back from the edge of oblivion. In the last five years alone, she'd already saved three museums from flat conversion, pulverization, extinction. Oakheaven was the latest on that list, so it would also be our home for the next eighteen months, minimum. And I was the one who'd chosen it.

From a short list of four museums that desperately needed Mum's help, Oakheaven was the only one that had grabbed my attention. I had returned to it again and again, the name tugging at my insides every time I'd heard it, until I'd finally given in to the strange curiosity that haunted me, and nagged Mum to take the job here.

I had made this unsettling day happen.

Annie Hoad has been dreaming about living in a castle since she visited a really cute one, when she was a child, and decided it would be a much more exciting place to live than a bungalow. Sadly, she still lives in a flattish sort of house, but her dreams of becoming a castle-dweller will never die.

She would like to thank Mr. Martyn for his amazing cover design, for the lovely chapter headings and his interesting choices in music. She would also like to thank her mum for reading this book many more times than she bargained for, her dad for his French translations, her sister for her T.A.T.W.A.F, Dotty and Donny for plot discussions, Anne (other) for her endless enthusiasm, Emma for always being so encouraging, Heather for the lovely long letters, and her cat for the company.

xxxx

Made in the USA
Middletown, DE
26 July 2020

13713688R00099